Love & Revolution

MODERN CHINESE LITERATURE FROM TAIWAN

Love & Revolution

A Novel About
Song Qingling and Sun Yat-sen

Ping Lu

TRANSLATED BY NANCY DU

Columbia University Press *New York*

Columbia University Press
Publishers Since 1893
New York   Chichester, West Sussex
Copyright © 2006 Columbia University Press
All rights reserved

Columbia University Press wishes to express its appreciation for
assistance given by the Chiang Ching-kuo Foundation
for International Scholarly Exchange and Council for Cultural Affairs
in the preparation of the translation and in the publication of this series.

Library of Congress Cataloging-in-Publication Data

Lu, Ping.
Love and revolution : a novel about Song Qingling and Sun Yat-sen /
Ping Lu ; translated by Nancy Du.
p. cm. — (Modern Chinese literature from Taiwan)
ISBN 0-231-13852-0 (cloth : alk. paper)
1. Song, Qingling, 1893–1981—Fiction.
2. Sun, Yat-sen, 1866–1925—Fiction.
I. Title: Novel About Song Qingling and Sun Yat-sen.
II. Title.   III. Series.
PL2880.U1646L68   2006
895.1′352—dc22   2006009064

Printed in the United States of America
Designed by Milenda Nan Ok Lee

c 10 9 8 7 6 5 4 3 2 1

CONTENTS

PREFACE

During the years I spent writing this novel, I felt as if I were caged by the confines of my imagination.

According to a story by the Argentinean writer Jorge Luis Borges, in the thirteenth century there was a savage leopard that stared at the walls of his cage all day long. He felt he was suffocating, and anguish churned inside his body with every move. One day he had a dream in which God appeared before him. God said to him, "You shall live and die in this prison, so that a man that I know may see you a certain number of times and never forget you, and he will put your figure and your symbol into a poem, which has its exact place in the weft of the universe. You suffer captivity, but you shall have given a word to the poem." In the dream God illuminated the animal's rude understanding, and the animal grasped the reasons and accepted its fate, but when it awoke it felt only an obscure resignation, a powerful ignorance, because the machine of the world is exceedingly complex for the simplicity of a savage beast.

In the same way I cannot recall for the life of me what prompted me to choose such a difficult subject and write a novel about it.

Wasn't my goal simply to take the last few months of Sun Yat-sen's life and turn it into a novel? Yet the years I spent writing the book were as arduous as any revolution. Night and day I pored over books on contemporary Chinese history and condensed information time and again in the hope of piecing the backdrop of the story together. I traveled as far as I could to search for clues to what took place during those final years. I went back and forth to Shanghai, conducted interviews in Beijing to understand all aspects of Song Qingling's life, including the loneliness she endured as a widow and in her solitary old age. I visited Hong Kong and Japan and read archived newspapers at the Library of Congress in Washington, D.C. I even stumbled across aspects of their story in Moscow. My goal was for the novel to have the appeal of fiction where imagination colors in the blanks left by history while remaining true to the facts. When it came to facts, the challenge I gave myself was that no one could dispute any of the historical data I included in the novel. Shut away in my study for days on end, surrounded by volumes of clippings, annals, and memoirs, I scoured the sea of documents. Gradually, as time passed, these figures from the past came alive for me. I was able to point to each person in an old group photograph and identify the faces without hesitation. I sifted through the maze of information and found common threads, areas of ambiguity, and a chronology of events. As in a jigsaw puzzle, I had to test how every piece of information fitted: Why were people present at the same historical meeting recounting distinctly different perspectives? As the story came into focus, I began to understand how political inclination and life choices ultimately determine facets of individual memory.

What happened all those years ago? What actually happened? Like a person obsessed, I searched for the truth. If I had to cross the river to Hades to bring the souls of the protagonists back, I would. When I came to the final chapters of the book, I was suddenly gripped by dread. I did not want to let them go; I feared separation from that world, as if I were being abandoned to a solitary existence on Earth.

From preparation to completion the novel took me seven or eight years to write.

Like the leopard in the dream, I felt that God had tried to impart something important to me through the writing of the book, but I have since forgotten the meaning. Rather than say I wrote the book, in the end I see it as the book writing me.

Even now I cannot quite explain why I stubbornly persisted in putting this tumultuous story down on paper. The story still cannot be published in China, where it is set, as it touches on the private lives of revered comrades. In Taiwan, because Sun Yat-sen established the Republic of China in 1911 and political tensions across the straits remain intricate, the story is definitely not politically correct.

Preface

Yet a few years after the Japanese version was published, the English version is now coming out. I am grateful to the translator, Nancy Du, for giving the book a second lease on life that allows it to meet a wider audience. I would also like to thank Professor Chi Pang-yuan and David Wang, who pushed so hard for the English version. Their tireless efforts have allowed the central characters of this novel, Dr. Sun Yat-sen and Madame Song Qingling to finally come face to face with the Western world.

BRIEF BIOGRAPHIES OF SUN YAT-SEN
AND SONG QINGLING

Sun Yat-sen (also known as Sun Yixian, Sun Zhongshan, and Sun Wen, 1866–1925) is considered the founding father of modern China, both in the People's Republic and in the Republic of China (on Taiwan).

Born in a peasant family in Cuiheng, Guangdong Province, Sun was sent to join his older brother in Hawaii in 1879. In 1886 he began his medical studies, and in 1893 he began to practice in Hong Kong. Sun was still a student when he began to take a serious interest in China's political affairs and to entertain ideas of overthrowing the Qing dynasty. In 1894 he organized his first revolutionary group, the Xing Zhonghui (Revive China Society), composed mainly of members of secret societies. After a failed uprising Sun became a professional revolutionary; he had to leave Hong Kong and sought refuge in Japan.

From abroad Sun tried to keep the revolutionary movement alive. He became a fund raiser for revolution, seeking support from overseas Chinese communities all over the world. During one of his trips, to England in 1896, he was kidnapped by agents of the Qing government and held captive in the Chinese legation. Dr. James Cantlie, a former professor of Sun's, intervened and managed to secure his release. The incident gave Sun an international reputation as a notorious revolutionary. Sun, in the meantime, was setting up branch organizations in Europe. In 1905 he was elected the director of the Tongmenghui, a more centralized and carefully organized revolutionary league based in Tokyo. Students and young intellectuals formed the core. Sun's Three People's Principles (*Sanmin zhuyi*)—

nationalism, democracy, and the people's livelihood—were incorporated into the league's constitution.

By 1909 Sun had become persona non grata in most of East Asia. This was why he was in the United States, raising money, when the Qing dynasty fell in 1911. Instead of returning to China immediately to head the revolution, he went to Europe to explore diplomatic recognition of and foreign loans to the new government. He arrived in Shanghai in late December 1911, and on January 1, 1912, he was inaugurated as provisional president of the Republic of China. In early February 1912 Sun resigned in favor of Yuan Shikai, the former military strongman of the Qing. In an attempt to regain power through the newly active National Assembly, Sun revamped the Tongmenghui, together with other progressive parties, into a new political organization, the Nationalist Party. In 1914 he married Song Qingling, although his first marriage had not been officially annulled.

Given Yuan Shikai's penchant for assassinations of political adversaries and assemblymen, relations between him and Sun deteriorated. In 1917 Sun left for Canton, where he convened a rump parliament and established a military government. He was supported in this endeavor by the local warlord Chen Jiongming. But Chen and Sun had a falling-out, and Sun was expelled from Canton in 1922. While in Canton, Sun had established contacts with the Moscow-based Comintern. After discussions with various Comintern representatives, including Henk Sneevliet (Maring), Chicherin, and Adolph Joffe, Sun decided to align the Nationalist Party with the Soviet Union and the fledgling Chinese Communist Party, and to reorganize the Nationalist Party. This turned it into a tightly disciplined party organized along Leninist principles; the Three People's Principles remained the basic aims. The Soviet Union supplied money, weapons, and advisers to secure both military and political support for the Nationalist Party.

On March 12, 1925, Sun died of liver cancer. After the Nationalist Party government was officially established in Nanjing in 1927, a personality cult of Sun soon pervaded the country. In 1929 his coffin was entombed in a massive marble mausoleum in Nanjing. In 1940 the Nationalist Party decreed that Sun should be revered as "father of the Republic" (*Guofu*).

BRIEF BIOGRAPHY OF SONG QINGLING

Song Qingling (also known as Mme Soong Qingling, 1890–1981) was born into a wealthy Christian family that played an important role in Chinese politics in the first half of the twentieth century. Qingling and her sister Ailing studied at the Wesleyan College for Women in Macon, Georgia; their sister, Meiling, attended Wellesley College in Massachusetts. Qingling married Sun Yat-sen in 1915, whereas Ailing married the banker and political figure Kong Xiangxi, and Meiling married Chiang Kai-shek.

As the widow of Sun Yat-sen, Song Qingling became an important member of the elite of the People's Republic of China (PRC). She was present on the Tiananmen rostrum when Mao Zedong delivered his speech inaugurating the PRC in 1949. But despite her elevated position and high political visibility, she was officially inducted as a party member only one week before her death.

Although she was a vice chairperson of the People's Republic, her influence in political matters was limited. Instead, she busied herself with various welfare activities, ranging from heading the Women's Federation to working on a number of committees involving orphaned children.

TRANSLATOR'S NOTE

As the story opens, Dr. Sun and Song Qingling are leaving Kobe, Japan, for Tianjin, China, and then to Beijing where Dr. Sun hoped to hold a National Congress meeting and call for the abolition of all unfair treaties with the Western powers. They had left China two weeks earlier via Shanghai to hold peace talks with the northern regional leaders on the unification of China. Dr. Sun toured Japan with stops in Nagasaki, Kobe, and Port Moji so he could gain the support of the Japanese people in opposing European hegemony.

Love & Revolution

Dr. Sun Yat-sen's last voyage was unforgettable. If there must be a beginning, look at the photograph taken on deck. The photograph was taken on November 30, 1924. An aide had glanced at his pocket watch as the shutter clicked—three minutes to ten. This memorable snapshot was recorded aboard the *Hokurei Maru,* before it left Kobe.

In the photograph Dr. Sun wears a look of sadness and gravity. He has on a padded mandarin gown and a short overcoat. In his one hand he holds a gray felt hat, and in the other he loosely cradles the head of his cane. Two weeks earlier, on November 17, he had arrived at the port of Shanghai. A reporter for *Wen Hui Bao,* the local newspaper, had written, "Dr. Sun appears older by the day. He is a different man from the one I met in 1921. His hair is grayer and he lacks his former luster." On December 4, four days after the photograph was taken, Dr. Sun disembarked at his destination, Tianjin. The newspapers in Tianjin described him as "of swarthy complexion . . . a dappled head of white . . . no trace of his old self." The truth was that, since the start of this trip from Japan, journalists had used variations of the same adjectives to describe his dejected appearance. Some newspapers even sneered that Dr. Sun's health had deteriorated because he had married such a young woman.

On closer inspection this photograph of Dr. Sun at the Kobe Harbor exemplifies that contrast. Song Qingling is standing right next to Dr. Sun, her head slightly tilted. She has on a fur hat and a gray opossum coat. Her feet are ensconced in a narrow pair of pointed high-heeled boots. Upon second look, one notices the almost frown on her face that makes her appear melancholic. She reminds one of a young bride, her heart slightly aquiver.

In the next instant, perhaps because he had caught sight of the distant Liu Jia Mountains and remembered the days of his youth, Dr. Sun walked toward the bow of the ship. Looking far older than his years, he stood against the light so that a dark shadow stained his forehead. His expression was indiscernible, giving no hint of what was on his mind. When one pores over the records of that fateful day in the official Nationalist Party records, the only clue lies in the phrase "Dr. Sun stands for a long time at the bow of the ship, takes off his hat and acknowledges the crowd." The two volumes of these records are as heavy as bricks and contain all the blood, sweat, and tears of the movement that immortalized Dr. Sun, yet his followers omitted all mention of the restless and romantic nature of revolutionaries. For example, Dr. Sun could slip from glee to gloom in an instant, and he loved to dream. The Peoples' Congress that he was intent on establishing was only one of his many dreams. Kobe, the city from which the ship was departing, was where his dreams had been born. His turbulent life was irrevocably tied to the tide of contemporary Chinese history. Even so, he cared greatly about what others thought of him.

At the precise moment the picture was taken, however, Sun Yat-sen felt quite pleased with himself. Although Inukai Tsuyoshi, the Japanese politician, had yet to meet up with him, and Sun Yat-sen had not been invited to Tokyo, his speech on Pan Asia the day before at the girls' high school was already headline news in Kobe. The newspaper *Asahi Shimbun* in Osaka also gave him a half page, which meant the paper still cared about what he was doing.

> Be a defender of the Kingly Way of the East,
> Or a lackey of the Western reign of might?

He murmured the beautifully rhymed couplet to himself—how the words rolled off his tongue. He raised his arm as he faced the crowds, which were like countless ribbons about to be torn from him. Each time he departed from a harbor he was never sure he would return. Perhaps this time more than any other. . . . Before he left China, he had prophesized his fate. During the farewell dinner at the Whampoa Military Academy, Dr.

Sun had mentioned that he did not know whether he would return. He said he was already fifty-nine years old, so he was not too young to die. For the last few months he had been able feel his organs rapidly giving way. His old friend Akiyama Sadasuke had advised Dr. Sun to move to Kyushu to recuperate at the hot springs resorts, but how could he leave with the country in the state it was in? Anyway, the word *recuperate* had never been part of his vocabulary. Even with his days numbered, his political instincts told him to make the most of the time he had left. Before leaving, he had reiterated with fierce conviction, "If I cannot go north, I'd rather die!"

The ship began to rock. In his cabin Dr. Sun was famished. Even though his eroded stomach could take only a little soup, he still managed to spoon bits of seaweed into his mouth. He had always preferred lightly seasoned Japanese cuisine but was unaccustomed to slurping his soup. Fifteen minutes later his aide, Ma Xiang, cleared the table and was happy to see the soup bowl empty. He wanted to help Dr. Sun retire for the night but heard Sun telling Dai Jitao, the only comrade on board who was not seasick, how he had escaped to Kobe with his childhood friends Chen Shaobai and Zheng Shiliang after the failure of the first Guangzhou Uprising. It was the first time the three of them cut off their queues. Dr. Sun started to say with a laugh, "In 1895," but before he could finish his thought, he saw his wife emerging unsteadily from her cabin. How old was she at that time? One or two years old? From the moment they joined as husband and wife, he knew she would end up widowed.

"Rosamund," he gently whispered her beautiful English name. With his eyes he beckoned to his tottering wife to come to his side.

Amid the fragrant smell of flowers I knew I should be content. Yet like a person who had been through too much, I found it difficult to believe my luck had turned. I kept reminding myself that this festively decorated room was not a dream.

In the afternoon, while Simpson's parents napped, I stepped into the bathroom that was like a greenhouse. I filled the bathtub, took off my clothes, and sank into the deep marble tub.

Sitting in the hot water, I felt my flesh dissolving inch by inch. I rubbed my eyes through the steam; I thought I could see snow outside on the lawn. My thoughts drifted back to those bleak days as I trudged down the back streets of New York and the snow came right up to my knees. Sometimes, when hail rebounded off my body, I almost believed the small beads of opaque ice had jumped out of my nostrils.

I reclined along the curve of the tub, and the backward motion of my hand set the water swirling. The water gently pushed, then pulled, me. The ripple of water in the sunlight cast a play of shadows before my eyes. I couldn't stop thinking of Madame's naked body in the water. Strangely enough, her body was still softly feminine at eighty. The breasts that hung from her were like a pair of gourds. Her shoulders sloped gently downward, sketching a beautiful arc from her neck down to her waist.

I had stared as her contour emerged from the steam. Her back was to me, and I saw the delicate mounds of fat on her back glistening like pale alabaster. It was as if the years had not left a trace.

I tiptoed back to the room wrapped in my bathrobe. As the door closed behind me, I glanced around at this home that seemed so castle-like to me. It was hard to imagine that one day all this would belong to Simpson and me.

I touched the round stool in front of the dressing table and sat down. Simpson's mother favored Asian designs. On one end of the room was a birdcage displayed against a box made of camphor wood. I put my cheek against the surface of the table and with my mouth next to the mirror blew a watermark.

I raised my head to look around the room. In addition to the birdcage, there was a red door curtain with mandarin ducks embroidered on it, a replica of a porcelain vase, a pair of dragon-phoenix lanterns, an opium pipe hanging on the wall, and the sound of wind chimes in the background. In the mirror I looked at my long narrow eyes. I would often bat them at Simpson and ask him coyly, "Who do you think I am?" He would always pinch my cheek and answer loudly, "You're my China!"

What about Madame Sun? For many years, if she had any friends at all, it was those foreigners. They called her affectionately by an English name; they kissed her cheeks, held her hand, and embraced her almost obese, bed-ridden body. But they didn't call her Rosamund; they called her "Suzy,"-- "Suzy! Suzy!" The two short syllables would work like magic: her eyes would suddenly open.

The night we moved into this festive-looking room, I had a dream. I saw my sister sinking very quickly. With my hand I tried to hold onto her but we ended up being entangled. We were sucked into the sand; our feet disappeared until finally only four flailing hands were visible. I began to scream. I woke up.

I saw Simpson sitting next to my bed with his worried and sympathetic blue eyes.

When Simpson held me in his arms, I remembered the night of Madame's funeral: my sister had knelt in front of my bed, pleading with me to leave quickly. Otherwise, there'd be no time, she'd said earnestly.

I couldn't see her expression because her hair had fallen over her face, but I could feel her nails digging into my flesh. With a quiver in her voice she'd urged, "Don't forget me when you live the good life abroad!"

At night he knew without looking that searchlights glittered in the distance. Like an experienced sailor, he could tell from the damp scent of salt that the *Hokurei Maru* was navigating through coral-filled waters. The bobbing of the ship pushed his thoughts to his base in the South. This was their seventeenth night at sea, and he imagined the harsh lights that would be emanating from the building on that darkened embankment of the Pearl River. After the revolt they had relocated to this former factory for safety. Its sturdy structure could defy gunfire, and the river was right next to it, so it was like having a moat. Each floor had a veranda with palm trees and bougainvillea encircling it. The professional boxers he had hired from the West kept vigilant watch between the trees. But as long as his wish to claim the North burned bright, the fortress seemed like a prison to him. "If I cannot go north, I'd rather die!" Although this kind of rhetoric sounded heroic and ambitious, he could already tell that Guangzhou was a dead end. The city where he resided had turned against the Nationalists. If he couldn't proceed north and push for unification, his life's work as a revolutionary would have been in vain.

In the darkness a spectrum of color shone from the searchlights. The concrete building he had inhabited appeared like a boat adrift on the Pearl River, far from any corner of the continent. This was exactly what he feared, not having a place to dock. A year earlier, when Chen Jiongming had betrayed him and surrounded the presidential office, he had been lucky to escape first. His wife, however, had had to flee, hiding like a fugitive among the pillars in the corridor outside his office. Ah, Rosamund . . . after their wedding, she had suffered ten turbulent years with him.

Lying next to him, she snored softly. Her breathing was even and steady; she was obviously in a dreamless state. He felt envious; she was young, after all—a few minutes ago she was still feeling seasick and now she was asleep. He rubbed his own eyes. Perhaps he couldn't sleep because of the dull ache below his stomach. But it didn't seem to be that, so he tried straightening his body. He could not see anything through the small porthole in his cabin. It was pitch black outside. He pressed his ear against the steel wall of the cabin; under the crash of waves he thought he could hear the sound of people being slaughtered. Dr. Sun suddenly recalled being adrift on the bloodied Seto Inland Sea. His thoughts turned to the situation in the north. The newspapers abroad had referred to the warring factions as "warlords." People who cut up and pillaged land, people who were no different from the Shoguns in Japanese history. What hurt Dr. Sun more than anything was how many viewed him as a warlord. The newspaper *Shen Bao* in Shanghai still referred politely to him and his wife as Mr. and Mrs. Sun, but the newspapers from other cities called him Canton Sun. That was no different from Manchuria Zhang. Ha, you are only seen as a leader of a local government, he mocked himself derisively. Dr. Sun had always set his expectations too high. He was making this trip up north even though he knew deep in his heart that it was an impossible mission. Did he even have an idea what his next step would be?

Dr. Sun tossed and turned in his bed as these thoughts flooded his mind. Suddenly, he grunted. Two nights before, when he had been lying against the back of a chair, he had felt the same excruciating pain. He put his hand on his stomach and lay flat on his back. Still in pain, he turned on his side again. Whatever happened, he was certain of one thing: he simply could not stand by and watch while others wrecked the country he had fought so hard to build.

The evening that Madame fell into a coma, we were forced to leave her bedside and move back to our own rooms. Somehow they knew she would not wake up. They mocked us with a "now let's see what will happen to you two" look in their eyes.

In the past it had been a well-guarded secret that the people who served her, the men and women who called her "Chief" to her face, did not like her. In fact, they detested, abhorred, and hated her. Their hypocritical faces made me shudder. They were all accomplices, accomplices in lies. . . . On the surface they served her, but in their hearts they hated her with a vengeance. As soon as she went into a coma, they took revenge on the two people she loved most in the world, the two of us.

My sister was indignant. With a sharp glint in her eyes she yelled, "Let's have it out! We are her daughters. That's what she tells everyone. She says we're family, we're her closest kin. What's wrong with that? What's more, everyone knows of her relationship with Papa, even our mother."

Later, they prohibited the two of us from going to the funeral parlor while people formed a line in front of her gravestone and paid their last respects. Everything they did was to protect her and her reputation, they said.

Madame Sun always hated this hypocrisy. Children she hardly knew circled her and called her Grandma Song. I felt like yelling, "Don't you know, whether they drew a picture of her or folded origami, they were forced to dedicate it to the *esteemed* Grandma Song?" Later on she lost the patience to even go along with the pretense.

"Dead or not, the show must go on," my sister spat out scornfully.

It was the most despicable lie.

At the funeral relatives whom we'd never met before, who had nothing to do with her, came to pay their respects. They were not from her family; they were merely very distant relatives of the Sun family.

When I went abroad a few years later, I came across what Harold Robert Isaacs, her treasured Jewish friend, wrote in his book: "I can testify that the authorities went against the wishes of Song Qingling. I can also imagine how painful it must have been for those two young girls. Madame Song told me quite frankly before her death that the only people she cared about in this world were those two little girls."

But we know that history continues to be filled with all kinds of lies.

The next morning he woke up to the bobbing of the ship. The racking pain that had kept him up all night seemed to be a distant memory.

He sat up and his eyes fell on his wife in the other bed. She looked so childlike with her body all curled up. Sometimes he imagined himself protecting her with every last ounce of strength in him, but that occasion had never arisen. He could not lie to himself; he knew that when the time came, he would probably still have to abandon her. During the fall of Canton it was Madame Sun who had stayed in the restaurant till the very last moment. It was she who experienced the fighting in the streets. The one common thread running through her many biographies was the mantra, "Yat-sen, China could survive without me but not without you." Each time she had insisted he go. During the fall of Canton Dr. Sun had narrowly escaped by masquerading as a doctor making house calls. He was wearing dark glasses and carried a medicine chest around his waist. When he left, he knew he might never see her again.

"Rosamund," he mouthed wordlessly, not wanting to wake his wife. Dr. Sun contemplated, quite uncharacteristically, how his young wife needed more sleep than a sixty-year-old man. Hovering by her bedside, he watched through myopic eyes her gently flaring nostrils and the fanlike shadow cast by her thick dark eyelashes. He cherished these intimate moments with her.

After some hesitation he thought of gently taking her hand, which was outside the blanket, and placing it against his wrinkled face. He started to reach for her hand and then stopped. At that instant he felt how politics had made him vile. But he knew this sense of disgust would not stay with him for long. Very soon he would be actively engaged in some other similar situation or responding urgently to some emergency.

He straightened his wife's blanket for her and gazed out the window. In the distance he could already see land; they would soon be arriving at the familiar Port Moji. He blinked his weary eyes and remembered how in 1918, while on the train from Hakone to Kobe, he had contracted conjunctivitis. At the time his eyes were so sensitive to light, they could not make head or tail of the images before him; he was aware only of the outline of trees as the train rushed by. Those were indeed miserable times. He was fleeing for his life, having been driven out of Canton by the warlord of the Gwei faction, and Chen Chunxuan, who was responsible for brokering the peace, had ordered that he take a trip abroad. Dr. Sun had taken the ship to Moji; even in Japan, where he had always had the most supporters, very few had shown up at the harbor to greet him. Only his most loyal friends, Miyazaki Enzo and Sawamura Yukio, were there. His wife had been in Shanghai for her father's funeral. She had been actively involved in negotiations with the French consulate about the fate of the French-occupied territories.

During the few days he had spent in Kyoto, he'd a chance for the first time in years to stop and listen to what his heart was telling him. His vision was impaired, but he could suddenly hear the sound of pine needles dropping on moss as well as the whisper of the wind as it rustled through the trees and shook the reflection of the trees over the face of the pond. For the first time in his life he wondered what he might have missed out on in the name of his cause. He would never again experience tender, quiet moments or sample the life of everyman. He recalled that the ophthalmologist in Kyoto was called Ichikawa; he also remembered that it had been around June when the weather was warm enough for him to wear just a lightweight shirt. He had seldom been ill. For revolutionaries a precarious balance existed between their spiritual and physical state. To fall ill meant one had lost that crucial tug-of-war. With great vigor he rubbed the sagging skin on his face with both hands. He sighed heavily. At that moment he realized to what extent politics had aged him.

Dr. Sun recalled that he had slept poorly the latter half of the night. He had had terrible nightmares. Perhaps it was because of the dull ache in his stomach, but the longer he was in bed, the more alert he became. He didn't want his wife, who was fast asleep, to have to worry about him. Only he knew about the dark premonitions he had been having lately. Very often the graver the issue, the more he hid it from her. It was as if he did not want the stubborn young woman to realize that he had always been the one who was better at compromising.

Comparing the two of them, Dr. Sun could not deny that his wife was the one who harbored qualities of perseverance and honesty, who stood by principles, and who plowed doggedly ahead in the name of her beliefs. Often, when Dr. Sun mentioned without much confidence some idea or policy he had thought up, he would be surprised at how quickly she would become his most ardent believer. He could not help but worry about her. Recently, he had wanted to tell her a few things: he wanted her to know that she should strive to be someone ordinary, that the revolutionary ideal was actually not that noble, and that the most treasured aspects of life were probably wholly unrelated to politics. But he had probably left it too late. He felt the pain grip his insides again. God might not leave him enough time to bare his soul to the last woman in his life. But perhaps more pertinent was that even if he had sufficient time, would he actually say those words? Perhaps it was his own selfishness, but he didn't want her to come face to face with the way the world was. He knew her love for him was tinged with adulation, and from the start her reverence toward him was what enabled him, a man much older than she, to win her heart. He was the first man in her life, but before her, he had had many women. But he valued her above all else. He would rather that she was a prized nightingale in captivity that knew nothing of the world. But what would happen afterward? Without his protection she would be heading into danger. Would she come across someone who was more deserving of her love and body at a later date? Staring at her soft, luminous skin with visions of that indeterminate future on his mind, the fifty-nine-year-old man could almost taste his unfounded but very bitter jealousy.

As I reclined in my chair in the afternoon, I had a dream. At first, everything was a blank canvas; then a feather floated gently down. People have said that in recent years it rarely snows in Beijing, do you believe it?

They locked up my room and my sister's room in the Houhai house. It was not on the visitors' itinerary because the two of us weren't supposed to exist.

A book written in commemoration of the life of Madame Sun remarked at the end, "a heroic heart finally stopped beating." I really had no idea that hearts came in the heroic and unheroic kind.

A moment ago, through the window, I saw workers putting up the wedding marquee on the lawn. In the blinding sunlight I was suddenly transported back to Tiananmen Square, where the swearing-in of the Red Guards took place right before my eyes. In my confusion I almost thought to start marching. When I reopened my eyes, I realized that what I had heard was only the sound of the football game being broadcast downstairs.

After I woke up, I sat up straight and looked at the row of perfume bottles lining the dressing table in the guest bedroom: Chanel No. 5, Joy, Poison . . . illusions of glamour that came in all shapes and sizes. Back in the early days she would often sit in front of her dressing table and finger the half-empty, evaporated, and almost forgotten bottles.

The list of wedding guests lay inside the silver fruit tray. The guests were all friends of the Simpson family, none of whom I knew. I remembered the mansion behind dense trees where Madame Sun's sister had lived. Once, someone had pointed her home on Long Island out to me as we rode past. So that was where the famous younger sister lived. Did that have any bearing on me now? After she passed away, it was not possible for us to have contact with any of her relatives.

I was reminded of the time when I heard that the Sun Yat-sen family was in a dispute with the Taiwan authorities over real estate. I bit my lip when I heard the news, and I didn't need to look in the mirror to know that I had a cold sneer on my face.

Bathed in the soft glow of the moonlight, I imagined myself as a bride in white. In one corner of the bed lay a big box that held the nightgown I would be wearing the next evening. It was from a shop called Victoria's Secret. I liked the name; it suggested something mysterious. The material was of the softest silk. In some ways I was a lot like Madame Song in our love of beautiful things.

I remembered seeing her after the Cultural Revolution. She had complained to us more than once that she was sick to death of the dull gray or blue suits she had been forced to don.

Once, I sat cross-legged on that big bed of hers and stared at a picture of her from 1945. She wore a polka-dotted *qi pao* and a pair of four-and-a-half inch stilettos. There was no way to tell she was already fifty-three.

When I secretly leafed through her photo albums, I saw pictures of her taken with Deng Yanda in Moscow. The Arabic numerals *1928* were written below the picture. Although it was the 1920s, they were so bold. They stood next to each other, shoulders faintly touching. She wore a sleek coat, and her round calves were casually placed one before the other. Her face was radiant and womanly. The picture actually reminded me of a song called "The Merry Widow." Deng, who looked very manly, had perhaps been her lover during those few years. I had heard others echo the same sentiment.

Could rumor be fact?

It was said that when she worked at the China Defense League, she had a close friend called Yang Xingfo. I knew that both Deng and Yang were killed during the civil war. Many years later she would still write articles commemorating their lives; it seemed that her sorrow for their loss never waned.

For someone who had been married for only ten years, how many lovers did she have in her lifetime? What kind of pleasure did they give her?

I couldn't stop thinking about it. I longed to know what kind of woman was Madame, or "Chief," as she was known to her subordinates.

On the other hand, it was almost impossible to imagine from my memory of my papa's bedridden and limp form how much he had once been in her favor.

I opened my eyes; I could not sleep anymore.

When the ship docked at Port Moji, Dr. Sun met with the local journalists in his cabin.

7

He had always been known for his quick wit. A few people had criticized him for being sly and chameleon-like. This may or may not have been true, but he was good at fielding on-the-spot questions from journalists. A reporter with short stubby whiskers suddenly asked him, "After you return to Beijing, who are you planning to nominate as president?" He replied in good humor, "Right now I am in Japan, so I don't have a clear picture from where I am to really say." He had managed to tactfully avoid embarrassment.

Dr. Sun took the opportunity to speak on something that was close to his heart.

This was an issue he could not be more familiar with: the abolition of the Unequal Treaty that Japan too had endured for the last thirty years. "The most important part of the message I bring is that we seek Japan's assistance in abolishing the treaty." His tone of voice quivered with the emotional urgency of an orator. "Thirty years ago Japan was subjected to the Unequal Treaty. My wish now is for Japan to do unto others as Japan would have others do unto her. I hope Japan can take the compassion gained from that heartfelt lesson in the past and support China in its current struggle."

When he spoke, his voice rang out loud and clear; his hands gestured emphatically. His conviction seemed beyond question. He especially enjoyed giving impromptu speeches because he felt he could effectively convey his revolutionary sentiments. To many, Dr. Sun's greatest strength was his verbal acuity. A founding member of the Nationalist Party, Zhang Shizhao, once remarked that when you were with Dr. Sun, you felt compelled to agree with him, even though you might disagree in hindsight.

At that moment, as he looked at the faces before him, Dr. Sun seemed to lose all traces of the fatigue caused by his insomnia of the night before. He felt a fresh surge of energy. He wanted, in the short space of time, to let them know the special significance that Japan held for him. He wanted them to know why he had once remarked, "We are like the reformers of the Meiji Restoration Period fifty years ago." It was the truth. Without Japan as his refuge, he would not have had the opportunity to rest and recuperate after his failed coup, let alone put together an organized group of revolutionaries. At the same time the Japanese had given him hope. If Katsura Taro had not died, Dr. Sun's dream of unifying China might have long been realized. Sun Yat-sen, however, was no longer an innocent. His many years as a politician had taught him just how utilitarian people like Inukai Tsuyoshi and Toyama Mitsuru actually were. Right from the start, he was only one chapter in their "China Dream." He was part of the militarists' plan to spread the risk, to place their eggs in more than one basket. However, Sun Yat-sen had his hopes. Right before he left for Japan, he had sent a coded telegram to Toyama Mitsuru and Inukai Tsuyoshi with this message: "Leaving Shanghai. Hope to meet at opportune time." During the journey he had wired another message: "Hope to salvage home situation. Going to Beijing via Kobe. Appreciate if could meet in Kobe to discuss circumstances in East Asia." Later, Toyama Mitsuru had made an appearance. He had arrived in Kobe from Tokyo and stayed at Sun's Toyo Hotel. But as soon as they started talking about the Unequal Treaty, they deadlocked. Toyama Mitsuru seized the opportunity to declare something like "Japan already holds special rights in Mongolia . . . when the situation in your esteemed country has changed for the better, when the threat of foreign invasion has been totally dispelled, Japan will definitely grant the return of Mongolia. If I were to abruptly concede to your demands, it would not be endorsed by the Japanese people."

Dr. Sun sighed at these memories. He gathered himself to field the next question. These young Japanese journalists were paler in complexion than the Chinese. They sported thick, black sideburns and moustaches. During a brief lull as the interpreter translated the question, he suddenly thought of his friend, the whiskered warrior Miyazaki Toten. Whatever the occasion, when the image of the warrior materialized in Dr. Sun's mind, he would think longingly of the life of a wanderer. When Dr. Sun's thoughts turned to

Toten, it was also the moment when his soul was at its most pure and sweet. If there was one friend he missed above all others, it was this man, without a doubt. The kind of mutual admiration that existed between men gave him great comfort, but as he gently wiped the sweat from his forehead, his mind turned to the other whiskered fellow, Huang Xing. He could envision the friendship between those two men as being even more selfless and absolute.

It was not the time to dwell on these thoughts any longer. He was only glad that Toten had already passed away so he would not have to see how Sun had smiled his way through countless political deals. No doubt, Toten would abhor his grimy, graying visage. Dr. Sun knew that Toten had engaged in a lifelong search for perfection; he hated any form of politics and yearned for absolute freedom, even though it did **not** exist. That was why he was an anarchist. If Toten could see him now—he did not want to think anymore.

Turning his attention back to the room, he was looking once again at these novice Japanese faces. He felt deeply frustrated—how could *they* understand the real importance of Sino-Japanese cooperation and the reasons why he had switched allegiance? After so many failed attempts at engaging Japanese participation, he was forced to admit that his strategy was a failure. It didn't matter how solid his relations with the Japanese politicians seemed, in the end they were only paying him lip service. To them there were only Japanese interests, and they placed their bets on both sides of the game. First they signed a secret agreement with Yuan Shikai, and then they signed a military treaty with Duan Qirei.

The journalists continued with questions about why Chen Jiongming had turned renegade and why peace could not be brokered between North and South. It was as if they did not know who he was. They were oblivious to the fact that Sun Yat-sen had finally stepped off his pedestal; he had put aside the glory he had gained in founding the Republic and had consented to go north. He could not shrug off his sense of defeat. The smell of gas fumes from the ship's engine mixed with the taste of bile in his mouth. He was forced to listen to questions from totally ignorant journalists on the issue of Guangdong. The hidden ache was still in his heart; he alone had to assume responsibility for the bloody massacre that occurred on that fateful afternoon.

Chief, they're destroying everything!

Chief, the West Gate and the city are at war. If you don't take immediate action, order will never be restored!

Chief, the shops in the city are threatening to go on strike!

He gave his orders with grave misgivings: if the situation had indeed deteriorated to that extent, they were to solicit the help of party officers and students for the army. If citizens refused to listen, the soldiers were to take the next step. . . . Later, when Dr. Sun looked at his own written orders, he could hardly believe he had issued such harsh commands in his own territory. What made it even more unbearable was that he realized he had acted no different from the ravenous land-hungry warlords. He knew this incident would always go down as a black mark against his name and he could not undo it. He remembered sending an urgent telegram to Han-ming immediately after he disembarked from the ship, reminding this loyal but obstinate comrade that from now on the people were not to be disturbed again.

8

I dreamed I was lost in the mazelike streets of Shanghai. Much of the city was shrouded in mist. I saw myself walking slowly up a flight of stairs. The door to my mother's room seemed to be open, or was it closed?

I also knew what connotations the word *Shanghai* held in English—to trick or force someone into doing something, to be more than sly, to use whatever means available to achieve one's ends.

Shanghai, I once said to Simpson, reminded me of rows of dusty French parasol trees, an old woman digging the dirt from under her toenails as she sat beneath the door of an old stone building, the peeling paint flakes from a ceiling scattered into bowls of congee, the sound of footsteps coming down a long and narrow staircase, bedpans being emptied right next to your feet, and the occasional pale face of a handsome, smiling man spotted on Nanjing Road. Of course, to any country bumpkin from Jiangbei, the term "a kept man" would inevitably surface.

What I didn't tell Simpson was in the eyes of Madame Sun: Shanghai was forever her one and only home. Her home was the white mansion on Huaihai Road. Even when the outside world was bleak and cold, inside her home the stoves were always warm. After Papa suffered his stroke, we were taken to Shanghai, where her home became our haven from the outside world. A big yard surrounded the house. I once found a couple of colorful croquet balls on the lawn.

Why didn't I talk to Simpson about it? I silently asked myself. Why have I chosen to hide this part of my childhood from him? Was it related to the sense of secrecy I detected all those years back? Was it that we were subject to great privileges and that people viewed us through different eyes, or was the reason a simpler one? I wanted to please this foreigner whom I was about to marry by seeing the city through his eyes, as an exotic place that colonialists had given up saving.

My memories of the days in Shanghai remained vivid. At the beginning of the Cultural Revolution, Madame Sun had left for Beijing. My sister and I stayed in a severely cramped half-bedroom with our mother. Our bed was a grass mat and a few wooden planks. My mother would writhe in pain on that bed or curse aloud with a hateful look in he eyes. Under the soiled mosquito netting she would first moan in agony and then shriek out, "Where is your father?"

I saw Papa in the hospital ward. I saw his limbs, dried and wrinkled by the wind. In my dreams Papa's dark brown genitals looked like shriveled prunes nestling between his legs.

After Madame passed away, I went to Shanghai to see Papa one last time. I remembered the smell of mildew that filled the ward. Papa's eyes resembled two hollow black pits. In my dreams they were two holes covered with spider webs. They give birth to some fat, soft maggots.

At the funeral we were allowed to look at her body only from a distance. Her face was all done up as she lay in the glass casket. Nearby a bunch of irrelevant school kids surrounded her to pay their respects. As the camera flashbulbs went off, one after the other, the children were told to squeeze out a few tears in an act of farewell. We were purposefully excluded from the funeral arrangements. We were not to be seen or heard. After she had fallen into the coma, the two of us were barred from her bedroom altogether.

Many years before, during the Cultural Revolution, someone had died in our building. The cause had been tuberculosis. With her hands clutching the window pane, Mama had told us disdainfully that the Shanghai custom had been to wrap a corpse tightly in a silk blanket. If this was not done, they believed moths would fly out of the body and enter another's nostril and spread the disease. Without reason, after her funeral, I had the same recurring dream. She was bound very tightly with a silk blanket, so tightly she couldn't move at all.

One summer years later, as I was sitting in our old house in New York, hundreds of termites crawled out from under the wooden floorboards. Staring at them, I could feel the hairs on my arm stand up and the tingling sensation of goose bumps. In my dream I saw myself squatting on the floor, laying eggs. The grayish mass started to crawl, straightening out its tails and turning into moths with flapping wings.

Sometimes, as I look into Simpson's blue eyes, clear as a cloudless day, I am reminded of Madame Sun sitting under the lamp. She did not want the dusty outer world of Beijing to taint her own spotless domain. She would sit very still, a woman past her eighties, and stare at the rainbow colors of the perfume bottles sitting on her dressing table. *The hidden scent of sleeves*—I don't remember where I came across that line.

I could imagine that her world must have been one of silence. She was left with only her memories. Many years later, in a tiny bookstore in Chinatown, I found a novel called *Love, Not to Be Forgotten*. I seldom read literature but this was a well-known love story. In it the main character would often see her mother pacing the floor at home. "*I thought it was just a funny habit of hers; little did I know she was actually communing with his soul.*" When I think back to Madame Sun's pacing her room late at night, I wonder with whom she was communing. I could only think it was with Papa.

When I am lost in reverie, a worried look clouds Simpson's clear eyes. He says jealously, "A penny for your thoughts!" My thoughts are like the jigsaw puzzles that occupy Simpson's mother. Little jagged pieces scattered all over the table while I tried to locate the one missing piece. Under the dim shadow of the lamplight, the image of Madame Sun's death slowly resurfaced.

For the next two days the sea was turbulent. In later years the only idea that people had of that period were the brief words "passing the Black Sea" recorded in history books. That afternoon, when Dr. Sun's Chinese secretary, Huang Changgu, approached him, he noticed for the first time how sick Sun Yat-sen looked. Huang Changgu sat down next to Sun Yat-sen and showed him a photograph he had kept by his side for many years. In the photograph Dr. Sun wore a midlength suit jacket with a white shirt and a waistcoat. He also had on a pair of pinstriped pants. Dr. Sun looked like a dandy, putting all his weight on one foot and seemingly tapping to the beat of an unknown tune with the other.

In the earlier years many were under the impression that Dr. Sun was not sufficiently dignified; this of course was an allusion to his relationship with women. The liveliest parts of Dr. Sun's face were his eyes. His penetrating stare captured the hearts of countless women, including the firstborn of the much-admired Song sisters. This aspect of Dr. Sun's life was a subject of contention among his comrades but at that moment, as Huang Changgu looked at Dr. Sun's gray, listless expression, he wished with all his heart that he could see Sun's eyes light up again as they once did when an object of desire was in sight.

Huang Changgu kept these thoughts to himself. He refrained from asking after Dr. Sun's health and attributed the fatigue to long-distance travel. The good news was that, in another day's time, they would be arriving at their destination, Tianjin. How could Huang know then that this would be the last place Dr. Sun would ever dock? No one knew how numbered his days were. To later generations, however, the most intriguing thing would be whether Dr. Sun, with his stunted political instincts, had foreseen the historical significance of his northern expedition. In other words, if Dr. Sun had not chosen to embark on this last journey, which was riddled with obstacles and danger, but had instead languished morosely in Guangdong, future generations may have seen him only as yet another thwarted leader from the South who had not managed to fulfill his dying wish.

Actually, at that particular moment not only were his kinsmen not aware of his place in history, but foreigners didn't think much of him, either. After the Western powers had carefully evaluated their own interests, they had decided again to jointly intervene in the affairs of China. China's only true ally seemed to be post-Bolshevik Russia. Not long after Lenin died, Dr. Sun had sent over a scroll with the elegiac couplet "*Our people have endured a hundred ills; / Your leader has suffered a thousand difficulties.*" Evidently, they were in the same boat. One really needed to have an understanding of the world situation at that time to grasp the predicament that Dr. Sun was in when he docked at Tianjin. After the First World War, the League of Nations had become a hollow shell; Mussolini had just emerged in Italy; Germany had just established the Nazi Party; Japan had endured a disastrous earthquake, and the man of the moment in the United States was President Calvin Coolidge. As for China, a state of anarchy seemed to prevail. Feng Yuxiang's betrayal dissipated Wu Peifu's aggressive move to unite the North and the South. Defeated, Wu had been placed under surveillance. Rumors abounded as to his whereabouts. Some said he was in Szechwan, others said he was seeking the assistance of Zhao Hengyi in Hunan. Even though the power of this warlord had been dismantled, many believed he was only waiting for the next chance. As for President Cao Kun, who was supported by the Chili Faction, he had been forced to abdicate.

On the day Dr. Sun arrived in Tianjin, the news broke that Cao Kun had attempted to poison himself in Beijing but had been saved at the last moment. In truth this was only a facade. Cao Kun's concubine had been as busy as a bee. She was actively trying to use her connections with the Zhang Zuolin faction to find a way out for Cao. In Zhungzhou war was also raging. Hu Jingyi and Han Yukun had decided to go to war over the disputed territory.

From the outside the political nucleus seemed to be calm. Visits to the countryside and talk of Buddhism seemed to be the tenor of the day. Duan

Qirei, whose ancestral home was Anhui, took to posing as a devotee of Zen and tea ceremonies. Even Feng Yuxiang, who had defeated Wu Peifu, was rumored to be embracing Buddhism. None of this could be considered good news for Dr. Sun. It meant that Feng's original resolve to collaborate with him had been weakened.

During this period public opinion in the North distrusted Dr. Sun's platform and ideals. Some newspapers even criticized Dr. Sun for not having the military strength of Zhang Zuolin and Feng Yuxiang or the reputation of Duan Qirei. They questioned the rationale behind his northward journey. "How can one who is ill-matched in power ask for equal rights?" Newspaper editorials mocked him for having "suffered too many blows so that only empty talk remained." They kindly suggested that he make "a graceful exit rather than hold on to a crumbling house of cards." Some articles pointed out bluntly that "Dr. Sun's ten years of struggle has come to naught because of his lack of power, so what good is his trumpeting of ideals going to do now?" They urged Dr. Sun to "step down while his name was still intact and enjoy his latter days in peace."

Looking back at this time, the foreign historian Harold Z. Schiffrin said it best: "The reason why Dr. Sun has always been regarded as a national hero was because the 25 years in which he fought for the cause were the darkest period in China's history. If he is taken out of the equation, that period would only have gotten darker."

The palace in Beijing felt cold and remote; its ceilings were too high. The huge, loftlike sitting room resembled the reception hall of a government building.

Sitting across from the two girls, Yuyu and Zenzen, she tried to recall the streets and sights of Shanghai. Lao Da Chang on Xiafei Road, the jazz notes from the Peace Hotel . . . she gave a start because she could almost hear the bells of Jianghai Gate tolling in the distance.

She remembered when she was newly widowed; the tabloids in Shanghai loved to print stories about her. She would complain in English to her Western friends, "So many rumored affairs, one man after the next; I wish they were true, even if just once, so I could at least say I got something out of it."

Which year had it been?

When did she decide she would no longer give up the happiness that was deservedly hers? S's washing her hair for her—she liked the feeling of S's supple fingers touching her scalp. S's hands were strong and powerful. As he moved his hands, she could detect the slight scent of sweat on his nimble hands.

What she loved most was the way he had brushed her hair. Her hair grew right down to her waist and was fine and soft as silk. When her hair was tangled in knots, he would get hold of a tortoiseshell comb and run it through her loosened hair once in the morning and once in the evening. It was as sacred as a ceremony. She slept with her hair down at night, and in the morning S would fix it into a tight shiny bun at the back of her head for her.

Each evening S would stretch his hands out and let her put hair balm into his palms. S would rub his two hands together and spread the balm evenly into her hair. After she washed her face, she would take a precious dollop of moisturizer and smooth it over her face. The last step before she switched off the lights was to cover the back of her hands and her palms with the Snow Cream lotion from Shanghai.

The first time she laid eyes on this man, who had been sent to be her personal assistant, she already fancied him.

S bent down to light her cigarette for her. Even though there was no wind in the room, he cupped his fingers into a small half-circle for her. She could feel the heat of his slightly curled fingers. She lowered her head in turn so as not to disturb the tiny flame with her breathing. If she had her glasses on, she would be able to see the fine hairs on the back of his hand. The hairs would have been magnified. The light of the match would have caught their youthful vigor. She had always preferred good-looking men. Sometimes, when she saw fresh stubble on the face of a young fellow, she could hardly contain her urge to caress it.

The few female secretaries sent over by the central government never stayed long in her service. Before you knew it, she would find some unpardonable fault with them and chase them away. In front of S, however, she never lost her temper.

Sometimes, when she was reclining in her bamboo chair, she would listen quietly to S's stories about the outside world. She would close her eyes and think in amazement how this man from the army had not only weathered the rigid system but had even managed to clamber to the position of personal assistant to a national leader. What effort that must have taken! Suddenly, their roles were reversed. She became the innocent young girl of old who cast her eyes adoringly at the man beside her, Sun Yat-sen. When they were newly married, she wrote a letter to a friend, saying, "Being married is like being at school, except there are no bothersome exams."

When she compared herself with S, who had gone from north to south with only a pair of grass shoes on his feet, she became keenly aware of how lucky she was. You really had to hand it to him; he was a quick learner. Before long, he could read her thoughts and think of all things related to her in this cagelike world. If S occasionally forgot something, she would pretend to be incensed.

The palm of her husband's hands, she remembered, was always cool to the touch. Perhaps because of his early years as a doctor, he tended to survey women with a cold clinical look of experience.

S's hands, in contrast, were warm and moist. After massaging her for an entire morning, drops of perspiration would ooze from his forehead and brow; they'd slide down along his hairline before dissipating like steam.

S was getting ready to hold her up for a walk; from a different angle it looked like they were walking side by side. She bent her elbow slightly for S to hold. When other people were around, she sometimes would appear less meek.

He gave her a reason to stay young. S taught her to pile her hair on top of her crown rather than wear the standard bun at the back of her head. She started doing things she had never done before. S would put his hands around her waist and tickle her, and then, like a naughty child, he would cross her arms at the back.

Before S came along, her wrinkled and saggy skin had been yearning for the touch of another person.

It wasn't easy handing herself over so completely to another person. She didn't do it as a child or when she was Madame Sun with a husband twice her age. Now that she was old, she had learned to surrender. She would ask S quietly what she should wear, what color scarf to use, who to see or not to see. . . . The important thing was, although she had seen much of the world, she wanted S to know that she really valued his opinion. She was trying her utmost to please a man thirty years younger than she. To her, this was the best experience of all.

When she saw S hovering about, she would be reminded of how her husband treated her in the old days. Both were young men just starting out: they were smart, diligent, and eager to learn. Nothing could compare to the joy of having a person of the opposite sex willingly hand over his or her young self to serve you.

When S wasn't looking, she would pick up strands of her own hair that had fallen around the bathtub—strands of white, limp hair with split ends that looked horrific clumped together. Quickly, she flushed them down the toilet. They recalled the years when she found those small hardened, yellowish crusts on her pillowcase with the two lovebirds embroidered on it. She couldn't contain her shock when she realized that the bits had come out of her own husband's nostrils.

He had used his fingers! Out of the corner of her eye, she would watch him like a detective, slowly passing her eyes over his liver-spotted hands.

She remembered seeing him stand in front of the mirror every Sunday morning with his chin tilted upward and a small pair of scissors in his hand when they were spending some quiet time in Shanghai. Did he use those same scissors to operate on his patients when he was a doctor? She would quickly avert her head in disgust. She wondered whether those sticky little things stuck to the ends of his nose hairs would give off an offensive smell.

Her husband's saliva had an unpleasant odor. During his last days a thread of saliva clung to the chapped skin on his lips with every breath he took. She remembered seeing how the saliva between his upper and lower lip lengthened and shortened, then lengthened and shortened. . . .

During those final days his skin had also grown clammy. One touch with her hands and it felt as if his skin would disintegrate and turn to powder. She couldn't shake off this feeling for a long time. . . .

When he was ill, she had a recurring dream in which a man's body turned into dust when she laid her hands on it. Her husband's lifeless eyes were like those of a dead fish, with too much white.

Even in her most bizarre dreams, an impulse would cross her mind. She really wanted to take Sun brusquely by the hand, dip his body into hot soapy water, and scrub him clean.

Suddenly, the image of his picking his nose emerged before her eyes again.

Which finger did he use?

She tried to avoid thinking about her own deterioration. Her hands, however, had been the one exception. They had stayed slim and elegant. She would first file the nails on her left hand, then, stretching out her right hand, she would nag S like a spoiled child to file the nails on that hand.

The *Hokurei Maru* docked in Tianjin on the morning of December 4. The comrades who had already arrived from Shanghai had arranged everything: Wang Jingwei jumped on a boat that took him to the mouth of the river, where he climbed on board to brief Dr. Sun on the situation in Tianjin and Beijing.

He listened attentively. Whether on account of the pain in his body or the string of bad news he was hearing, he seemed to be contemplative.

"No need to repeat that." Dr. Sun broke off the already short report with a wave of his hand. "The fact that they let us come already allows us to promote our goal."

After passing through the crowds of people collecting their bags in the main cabin, Dr. Sun put on his hat and left the cabin. The cold easterly wind blowing overhead reminded him that the last time he was in Tianjin was thirteen years before, in the heat of summer. He had just stepped down from his role as president. Back then Dr. Sun had wanted to devote his time to nation building so he had ceded his presidency to Yuan Shikai. Dr. Sun had stayed completely clear of politics and party matters. How naive he seemed in retrospect! He had believed that within the space of ten years the presidency was going to be Yuan's anyway. Dr. Sun had been so wrapped up in the construction of bridges and railways, innocently thinking that that was the only way to save China. He had earnestly hoped to bring stability to the country. He had felt that if Yuan Shikai's strength was in training soldiers, then why not let him train two million soldiers as the head of state? He himself would enter a different stage. He would put his mind to building the 200,000-kilometer railway in China. Thirteen years before, all he had wanted was for Yuan Shikai to let him manage China's national railroad construction plan. Intent on baring his soul to Yuan, he had boarded the *An Ping* cruise ship from Shanghai to Tianjin around the middle of July in the first year of the Republic.

Much had been said about that northward journey. Dr. Sun and Yuan Shikai had met more than a dozen times during that one month, each time for several hours. The result was that Dr. Sun had compromised and had been harshly exploited. He asked people on numerous occasions to trust Yuan and urged members of the Nationalist Party to "fully support the government and the president." He had a hand in consolidating Yuan Shikai's power; ironically, that also made it harder for him to overthrow Yuan later. The negotiations between the two men were not only a matter of political contention at the start of the new Republic but even now he still asked himself whether he had done the right thing. Should he have refused Yuan Shikai? Did he really have that option? For every honey-tongued flatterer who praised him for not holding on to power, there were other comrades who were baffled by his decision and asked why he had handed his presidency to Yuan on a platter. The truth was that Dr. Sun had sifted through all the political implications at the time and had arrived at this conclusion. First and foremost, he knew he was not good at details. He inherently disliked the trivia and boredom of administration. Zhang Daiyen had said, "Dr. Sun thrives on debate, but that is mainly the talent of an adviser rather than a decision maker." Unfriendly as this comment seemed, it held elements of truth. He was accustomed to expounding his views even when reality proved to the contrary. He would much rather be faced with an entire map of China, where he could boldly sketch his grand illusions, than with the truth. He was concerned that Yuan, who appeared to be in favor of his vision, would have his hands tied by the conservatives. Second, Dr. Sun actually had little choice. He had stepped down in part to gain Yuan's allegiance, but supporting Yuan was also his only alternative, given the financial quagmire in which the interim Nanjing government had found itself. The United League had all but dissolved because of infighting between the Hunanese and the Cantonese; worse still, nothing remained in its coffers to pay the soldiers. Dr. Sun had barely sat down in the presidential office in Nanjing when he was inundated by telegram after telegram asking for money.

Without pay the morale of the troops will be in danger; cannot be held accountable for their actions.

The interim government rushed to print $1 million worth of military paper bills that shopkeepers refused to accept; some rice shops even shut down in defiance. Dr. Sun had to resort to waiting for overseas loans. He sent urgent telegrams in quick succession, but it was Saturday and foreigners did not work over the weekend. He was forced to tell Huang Xing, who was coughing up blood from the stress, that the soonest they could expect a response would be two days later. Several weeks passed, and even when the presidential office finally shut down, they still had heard nothing from abroad.

Actually, Sun Yat-sen's government in Guangdong was still paralyzed with money problems. Ever since he dedicated his life to the revolution, his main function had been to seek funding from countries or from overseas Chinese. In other words, Dr. Sun reflected dejectedly, he had spent half his lifetime trying to raise money, while the other half, in his own words, was "devoted to abolishing the unequal treaties and fighting the oppression of imperialism." It would appear that his anti-imperialism mission had a direct bearing on his current predicament: a few days before he arrived in Tianjin, the French consulate had made it plain that Dr. Sun would not be permitted to pass through the French-occupied territories when he docked in Tianjin and he would not be allowed to host a welcome party at the Citizens Hotel in the French section. When he had stopped over in Shanghai on his way to Tianjin, the local English newspaper in the occupied territories also had tried to spread dissension among the residents in order to prevent him from stopping in Shanghai. When Dr. Sun's ship sailed into Tianjin harbor, many countries, with the exception of Russia, had formed a strong, united opposition against him. Of late, his staunchest enemy in the North, Zhang Zuolin, had also used this weakness to attack him. Zhang had publicly told reporters from the morning papers that "foreign diplomats in Beijing did not approve of Sun Yat-sen." Also during negotiations between Zhang Zuolin and Wang Jingwei, Zhang had openly challenged Wang by saying, "As long as you can get Sun Yat-sen to give up his pro-Russia actions, I, Zhang Zuolin, will personally ensure the foreign diplomats reconcile with him." Of course, this irony cannot be lost on anyone. Dr. Sun's knowledge of the affairs of the West had won him followers thirteen years earlier and was the main reason why old and young alike looked to him for leadership after the Wuchang Uprising. Now, a few years later, people who had stood by him were turning against him because of those same revolutionary ideals. That moment, as Dr. Sun stood by the shore, his heart was filled with sadness.

Several old acquaintances from before the liberation came to visit her in Shanghai. "Madame Sun, Madame Sun!" they called out after her. She looked at them through lackluster eyes and wished they would take their leave.

She had never been approachable. The many years she had spent alongside these friends doing welfare work seemed a distant reality. Her voice sounded distinctly hollow when she spoke to them.

Her "friends" seemed oblivious; they joked that in the whole of Shanghai, the only relics from the days of the occupied territories were the trees, the rows and rows of trees on the side of the road that were still called French parasol trees.

Xiafei Road, on the other hand, had long since been renamed Huaihai Road in memory of the Battle at Huaihai. She furrowed her brow as she struggled to remember. Like the name of the narrow road she had lived on, first with her husband and then by herself for many years, the name of Moliere Road had been changed, to Xiangshan Road in honor of the birthplace of her deceased husband; she, however, still preferred its old name.

During the last few years she had constantly reminded herself that all cities eventually deteriorate, just as all beauty inevitably fades. Still, she didn't have the heart to hear about the shiny walls of her city turning to dust. Mold, rust, and potholes now were everywhere; overgrown reeds as tall as she invaded mansion after mansion.

The irony was that her life mirrored the destiny of this city where communism had been born. Her great role had been in the occupied territories, in the colonies, in this lone haven of history; she had been told to never stop "sowing the limitless seeds of humanitarianism."

But right then, at that moment, she didn't know what she was supposed to be reborn as.

It was a particularly cold winter. In front of the fireplace she spoke to S about her former life.

Before the war with Japan, despite the evident dangers, she had helped sneak in such sympathizers as the U.S. journalist Edgar Snow and Dr. George Hatem, sending them to the red zone of Xianbei via routes that few used because they were so treacherous. They traversed border posts and endured inspections while they heard Nationalist fighter planes overhead dropping bomb after bomb. She remembered sitting in the living room of her home on Moliere Road, listening to accounts of how they hid in the basement, lying flat for two three days on end, not daring to utter a sound.

"They often heard the sound of footsteps coming from just above their cabins. Evidently, some sort of search was taking place with loud shouts and orders being barked out . . . when darkness fell, they swam to the shore of a nearby village and hid in an abandoned house," she told S. "A contact would come to meet them, and, upon exchanging signals, they would see commies with Mausers waiting to escort them."

S was unnerved by her accounts and asked for a cigarette. As she passed it to him, she noticed her round, manicured nails. Compared with the trials faced by her comrades, her life back home in Shanghai was, she had to admit, relatively tranquil.

Intermittently, she would let S know what a wonderful hostess she had been—not just with Dr. Sun but later, when she was widowed, she continued to host dignitaries from all over the world in her home. *Not just the ones you know*, she told S, *not only the likes of Kim Il Sung, Sukarno, and the chairman of the Soviet.* During those days, probably around 1945, *I believe it was September*, she even invited the two men who would begin negotiations with Chiang Kai-shek, namely, Mao Zedong and Zhou Enlai, to her house in Zhongqing.

Earlier still, she said as she looked into S's excited eyes, in 1933 she had even invited George Bernard Shaw, who had come to China for the first time, to her house on Moliere.

She reminisced with a smile, recalling that the reason she had invited the bearded Bernard Shaw to lunch was to solicit his support for the war against Japan. To that luncheon she also invited Lu Xun, Lin Yutang, Cai Yuanpei, Harold Isaacs, and John Smedley.

She raised her head and noticed the blank look on S's face. "Who was Bernard Shaw?" S asked her, a little shyly.

It's not important, you silly boy, she replied softly. It really is of no importance now. She stoked the coals in the fireplace and slowly slid her hands into the sleeves of S's padded mandarin jacket.

On an unusually warm October day in Shanghai, S played croquet with her on the lawn. She started out by teaching him the rules of the game, but before long he was playing better than she was. They made a bet: the winner could eat the chocolates her overseas friends had sent her. On purpose, S lost to her so she could have an excuse to indulge her sweet tooth. Her laughter rang loudly in every room of the house.

Her house was surrounded by high walls and a huge garden. It was like a hole in the earth, sheltered beneath the shade of leafy trees and totally separate from the outside world.

On the surface it seemed as if the men in power revered her as much as after liberation, but deep down she knew she was becoming more and more dispensable. During the first few years she was required to still make an appearance at state-held functions, but in the last year or two her role was solely to deliver a speech on June 1, Children's Day. Other than that, she didn't need to set foot out of the door or meet with anyone.

She was actually grateful for her present seclusion.

When other people were around, this person she cared about had to discreetly disappear. When an occasional visitor dropped in, she couldn't even speak to him. At most, she could only slip a note to S and leave it at that.

She knew that if she were not careful, wagging tongues would find her. It wasn't that she cared so much about it but rather that she worried that she would lose the chance to see S again. If any rumor got out, he would be charged. She didn't have the means to protect him. This realization upset her. It didn't matter what party was in power or how respected she seemed to be—when push came to shove, she had no means to save the man she loved.

She liked to play games with S.

When she saw the ball roll smoothly into the hoop, she would rush forward and clap her hands in glee.

She wanted only S by her side because only S could make her laugh.

She really didn't care about anyone else.

"Do you like this?" S whispered in her ear as he was giving her a massage in the morning. He leaned forward and pressed gently down on her rounded, almost indistinguishable, shoulder blades. S's large hands seemed to cover the curve of her waist.

"Tell me, do you like this?" S whispered again urgently. His voice cracked as if he were reciting the lines to a screenplay. He even trembled slightly, like a child who is treading in forbidden waters.

She murmured that in her life she'd never been this happy. Of course, that was not entirely true, but the words seemed fitting right then. Her mind was lucid, she had carefully used the words "my life" rather than the usual "during my sixty-odd years," the phrase she would use with friends when she wanted to emphasize her age. To mention the number sixty to S, who was barely thirty, would have ruined the moment.

She had always been on close terms with the literati. She was familiar with their mild manners and hesitant expressions as well as the inevitable cowardice they displayed when things came to a head.

She had rescued a lot of them. For instance, in 1933 she had to rally all over the place to save the likes of Ding Ling and Pan Zinian. In 1937 alone she had managed to save quite a few scholars, including some of the "the seven gentlemen"—Shen Junru and Zhou Daofen, as well as others. She had perhaps had contact with too many of them before liberation. She had spoken to them, visited them in jail, fought alongside them on different occasions, and attended their funerals; sometimes she had even felt their subtle, well-contained sense of admiration toward her.

She suppressed a smile to herself—probably because she could finally relinquish of her "interim mission." The kind of communication she craved today no longer had to be a true meeting of the minds.

This piece of land where she had dwelled thrived on volatility; campaign succeeded campaign, movement succeeded movement, all hurtling toward an inevitable end. Her mind anticipated the inevitability of disaster, an ending that was too painful for her to contemplate right at that moment.

She was *now in the habit of* or, should she say, she was *now habitually eager to listen for the sound of S's footsteps coming up the stairs each morning.*

It was a kind of inertia, a pattern all humans fall prey to—she didn't want to think any more, she was prepared to just live from day to day.

Adrift in this state of repose, she only prayed that these good times could go on forever.

After all, why should one try to reverse fate? What was there to put right, anyway? And even then, what next? From the beginning she had never been sure whether the world could ever conform to her ideals, and now she had all but lost faith in the notion.

She had heard stories of farmers who suffered terribly at the hands of landowners yet declined to utter any accusation at the perpetrators when liberation finally came.

"Perhaps they were just lazy," she told S languorously. They probably felt as lazy as she, mmm . . . too lazy even to turn **on** her back.

At noon the *Hokurei Maru* docked in the occupied French port of Mei-chang in Tianjin. The weather was freezing, but Dr. Sun still had on his long gown and mandarin jacket. He took off his hat and stood at the helm of the ship to face the crowds. Probably twenty to thirty thousand people were standing before him, periodically shouting, "Long live the Republic of China!" "Long live the revolution!" and "Long live Dr. Sun Yat-sen!" Amid the cheering, he escorted his wife off the ship.

Inside the cabin 500,000 toothbrushes were waiting to be unloaded. Every toothbrush handle had a picture of Dr. Sun and the title of commander-in-chief inscribed on it—he had ordered these when he visited the Shuang Lun Toothbrush Company in Shanghai. They didn't cost much and would come in handy as souvenirs for soldiers once the war was won.

Once ashore, he didn't stop for long. He climbed quickly into his car and went straight to the Zhang Yuan Hotel in the Japanese-occupied territory. Long before his arrival, banners welcoming him had already been erected in front of the hotel entrance.

At the steps to the hotel Dr. Sun, with one hand on his cane, stood in the middle of the crowd for a photograph. This marked the last group photograph ever taken of him. Mr. Li Yaoting of the Tianjin Tingchang Photo Salon took the photograph. At the time this photo studio, which had been in business for fifty years, also covered local news. This particular photograph was supplied to all the major newspapers in the area. Li Yaoting was the manager of the salon, and many celebrities, as well as prominent figures of the day, had posed for him.

Dr. Sun was on a very tight schedule that day. According to official records, at three o'clock in the afternoon he took a carriage to Cao Gardens to pay a visit to the warlord Zhang Zuolin. This was the last recorded time that Sun Yat-sen went out for an official meeting. Extant documents, all recorded within a few hours, reflect various versions of Dr. Sun's meeting with Zhang Zuolin.

History books generally like to quote an article written by a Beijing police attaché, Lu Zhunglin. He says Dr. Sun saw his upcoming meeting with Zhang as a daunting challenge. Sun's chief-of-staff, Li Liejun, had even referred to the meeting with the metaphor of attending "a banquet of no return." A great deal of thought had gone into picking the people who would accompany Sun Yat-sen; Wang Jingwei, Shao Yuanzhong, Li Liejun, and Sun Ke would make up the entourage. When the group arrived at Cao Gardens, Zhang played haughty and refused to come out to welcome them. Sun and his aides had to wait a very long time in Zhang's sitting room before the meeting took place. When the two finally met, an eerie silence ensued that was broken only by Sun's Cantonese-accented words of congratulation to Zhang for his defeat of Wu Peifu's faction in Hebei. On hearing this, Zhang appeared impassive; he seemed to insinuate that as an outsider Sun was not entitled to offer these congratulations. Apparently, after two coughs Zhang had arrogantly replied, "There is no need for congratulations when we are fighting among ourselves." Then Li Liejun, who was familiar with the ins and outs of the factions, tactfully interjected a few words of validation and this, supplemented by Sun's remark that "since the founding of the Republic, General Zhang has been the only person who has warranted face-to-face congratulations from me," defused a potentially tense situation. The host then invited the guests to drink some tea. Two other accounts offer rather different versions of what happened during this brief interlude as the guests raised their teacups. According to an article by the author Yang Zhongzi, "The two sides chatted amicably, Zhang kept raising his teacup and urged everyone to drink tea. He indicated he was willing to cooperate with Dr. Sun." However, according to Lu Zhungling's version, "at this time, Zhang raised his teacup and Sun understood this gesture signified an end to the meeting. He got up and shook Zhang's hand in parting."

Dr. Sun's personal aide, Ma Xiang, on the other hand, had a totally different account of the events that day. In his article entitled "My Northbound

Journey with Dr. Sun," Sun did not meet with Zhang that afternoon; rather, their meeting occurred three days after Sun arrived in Tianjin. During that visit Dr. Sun was accompanied solely by Ma and another aide, Huang Huilong. The day after the two met, Zhang even went so far as to visit Dr. Sun, repaying the courtesy. When Zhang arrived, twenty-odd cars pulled up next to Dr. Sun's hotel and more than a hundred guards stood waiting. The two met for more than three hours. Zhang was courteous and respectful toward Dr. Sun, and the substance of their talk was also vastly different. Ma remembered Zhang's expressing a sincere desire to follow Dr. Sun; he was even willing to assume the role of brigadier general under Dr. Sun.

What actually took place between Dr. Sun Yat-sen and Zhang Zuolin will never be fully clear. After so much had happened, people's memories were affected more by their own political inclinations than by what really happened. Take Lu Zhunglin, for example. He was an important general in the army from the Northwest, one of the first veterans to fight in the war against the Chili faction. Naturally, he harbored no favorable feelings toward Zhang, the leader of that faction. Descriptions of Zhang's rude arrogance accurately reflected Lu Zhunglin's personal view of Zhang. Lu himself was actually in Beijing when the meeting between Dr. Sun and Zhang took place. When Lu finally met up with Dr. Sun, it was twenty days later, upon Dr. Sun's return to Beijing. In his article, "A Record of Dr Sun's Northern Expedition," written many years later, Lu acknowledged that some parts of his report were derived from accounts given to him by Dr. Sun's aides. Lu made allowances for the accuracy of the accounts by stating upfront, "Forty years have passed since these events transpired. Inevitably some facts have been distorted, even forgotten. Some records are limited by what information was available; therefore, one must understand that discrepancies may exist." As for Ma's perspective of Zhang's swearing his allegiance to Dr. Sun, Ma had been a follower of Dr. Sun's most of his life. As an overseas Chinese well versed in martial arts, he was fiercely loyal to Dr. Sun, and it wouldn't come as a surprise if his memories were tinged with feelings of undying affection for Dr. Sun.

From Dr. Sun's own perspective, these details mattered little. Time and again, the gang of aggressively armed warlords had fooled him. He harbored no illusions about them; his meeting with Zhang Zuolin was just part of the pretense. What really concerned him were the white banners that he saw dotting the streets on his way from the dock to the hotel, protesting his arrival in Tianjin and his collaboration with the warlords. Who had put up these banners? It didn't sound like people from the enemy camp; instead, they had the ring of Nationalist Party sympathizers. If that were the case, it meant even supporters of the revolution in the North disagreed with his decision to negotiate with the warlords. Before he left for this trip Ding Weifen and Zhang Ji, as well as other comrades, had tried to talk him out of his abrupt decision to go north. What upset him were the rumors that he was making the trip up north so he would not have to relinquish power. Just before he left for the North, Dr. Sun had written a letter to Duan Qirei to let him know of his desire to go abroad for rest and recuperation after this journey. During his public appearances on the trip Dr. Sun had also reiterated that once the political situation had stabilized, he would be traveling to Europe and the United States. For fear of being called a liar, he had even stated that his departure would be around spring of the following year. After he arrived in Tianjin, he went so far as to issue an official declaration that he did not covet any kind of power or wealth.

Under the fading light of day Dr. Sun sat in the carriage leaving Cao Gardens with thoughts of retirement on his mind. He felt tired and defeated. He had visions of taking his wife to places he had visited before; they could go on a cruise to the United States or to Europe. They would be able to stand shoulder to shoulder by the ship's railings and admire the setting of the round sun over the flat horizon in the distance.

He was torn because he did not know the outcome to his present predicament. Worse yet, his dreams of nation building had not had the chance to materialize. Dr. Sun knew that even if he was sailing on a vast ocean with no view of shore in sight, he would not be able to pretend that none of this mattered to him. He simply could not sip from a wineglass, embrace his wife, and watch the setting of the sun as if he had not a care in the world.

At around five that afternoon Dr. Sun's carriage returned to the hotel. His face appeared a waxen yellow under the light. He held on tightly to a chair to ease himself onto his bed. He could not stop shivering; he whispered all the while that the area around his liver hurt. He had never felt such excruciating pain. After a sharp intake of breath, he asked his wife to apologize to the crowds on his behalf. He would not be able to attend the welcome party hosted in his honor in the downstairs ballroom.

She liked to hear S's stories about being taken prisoner. When he spoke, the inflection of his voice resembled the northeaster from his hometown, raspy and harsh, sweeping past boundless fields of sorghum. Although the image he painted was foreign to her, she could feel the bitter isolation he was describing.

"It didn't matter where they caught you; with a gun against your head, your only choice was to march toward the firing line," S told her with an audible shudder.

Watching his face and sensing his awe at having so narrowly escaped death, she couldn't help but see the bleak picture that still lay before him. Poor boy, there was no future ahead of him. S had powerful, muscular arms but a flat backside—a telltale sign he would be down and out on luck.

After the massage she touched his sweat-filled shoulders. In the depths of her heart she lamented not just the inevitable end awaiting him but also that she wouldn't be able to save him. On a certain level she couldn't even save herself.

She insisted on listing S as one of the editors of a book commemorating her deceased husband. In another book chronicling the life and times of her deceased husband, she also suggested S's name be used in the preface. It was the highest honor she could grant him in her current situation.

She wanted to let S know how she felt. In her mind the two of them were already inseparable. She often contemplated apologetically how little she could give back to him.

Her thoughts strayed as she waited for S to come up the stairs again. She narrowed her eyes and wondered what life would be like beyond these tall walls.

If they weren't so far apart in age, would she rather have remained by S's side and lived the life of an ordinary couple? In the mornings she would have to hurry to the markets with her shopping basket and at noontime . . . *what would she do around noontime?* Suddenly she had a hard time recalling, as she did not actually know that much about ordinary people's lives. She didn't even know where she should start her imaginings.

Not just her—in the Song family not one of them had the luxury to live the life of an ordinary person. None of them could escape, she thought in despair, the historical rhythm of birth!

One day S, the man with the long arms and legs, suddenly stopped joking with her and asked gravely, "We're in the new world now, so why don't we just go ahead and register our marriage?" She raised her head without saying a word. With great tenderness she let him know she would have been willing.

She stared at the dying embers in the fireplace. Her home had become a lone island with no outside support. Men who took care of her could easily become like dead leaves, swept to the side of the road and discarded.

Once she had tried earnestly to address the situation, but Prime Minister Zhou Enlai had turned her down.

She almost blurted everything out to him—she told him she longed to be a free person with the right to marry again.

But the prime minister was too smart for her. "Let's keep things the way they are," he said. She opened her mouth slightly in protest but no sound came out. What could she say to rebut that flawless piece of logic?

She looked into Zhou Enlai's eyes and saw the unspoken message; she felt a little disappointed at first but then, without an outward trace, she started feeling happy too. At least she now knew, in the short time ahead, that he was silently granting her his consent.

Her request to Zhou was designed to lay the groundwork so she would be able to protect S.

Titles mattered little to her. The word *husband* sounded hollow to her ears. She had been a widow for thirty years, but her married life had taken up only ten years.

She did not need a husband in name; she only wanted reassurance that this person next to her would be fine without her. At that second her heart was filled with tenderness toward S. Was it simply because he had no inkling of what the future held for him? It was a kind of naive ignorance, not knowing that the sky was about to cave in. As smart as S was, how could he know what destiny had in store for him? How could he possibly predict it? Their good times were numbered, this much she knew. The "Great Collapse" that she didn't need or want to witness was right around the corner.

The famous German doctor Schmidt examined Dr. Sun. The symptoms suggested a bad bout of flu. With some effort Dr. Sun raised himself up in bed and looked out the window. It was a December afternoon, and the sunlight seemed watery and ineffectual. Madame Sun had yet to return from a luncheon held at the residence of Li Yuanhong in the British-occupied territory.

Dr. Sun got to his feet and looked about for his spectacles. For years he had been a voracious reader, but lately his eyesight had started to fail him. He read to put ideas into practice. He read books on law and economics, constantly weighing ideas to see what foreign institutions would prove applicable to China. The one book he never grew tired of was Napoleon's biography. Whenever he read the passage on Napoleon's crossing of the Alps in the 1800s, he would be inexplicably moved. That poor lad from Corsica, who had suffered only defeat and setbacks before 1793, managed in the next twenty years to have Europe's entire fate tied to his own. That thought stirred Dr. Sun. When his eyes skimmed the part about the citizens of Moscow setting fire to Napoleon's home, he sighed and threw down the book in dejection.

Dr. Sun put on his spectacles and picked up the newspaper that was lying on the coffee table. It was the first time in two days that he could muster enough energy to skim headlines. It was all about factions that were seizing the opportunity during the cease-fire to privately recruit more men. One article mentioned that Wu Peifu had relocated to Ji Kong Mountain and was in the throes of battling a rare disease. Feng Yuxiang, on the other hand, seemed to be busy raising money for his trip abroad. He had already managed to raise $40,000. In the next instant Dr. Sun smirked. The *Guangdong Sun* in one article was alluding to none other than himself. The *Sun Command Center's* article had news about the movements of his base in Guangdong. Mention of the members of the "People's Party" were referring to his beloved comrades . . . even his arrival in Tianjin two days before warranted a few words in the Comings and Goings column.

On the next page he read that someone in the United States had invented a new motorcycle designed to escort criminals to jail, Mussolini had plans to recuperate on the island of Sicily. . . . Near the edge of the page, mixed in with the jewelry ads, was a section about all sorts of Chinese herbal medicine and ointments guaranteed to cure stiff joints, ensure longevity, enhance sexual prowess, and inject stamina. . . . It was almost impossible to distinguish between what was considered advertisement and what was news—a testament once again to the lack of scientific spirit in Chinese people. One would be hard put to understand the progress of industrialization in the North just from the coverage in the newspapers. Perhaps the sizable article about the canned stewed beef being manufactured by the Taikang Company from Jinan was proof that advanced food processing was still in its infancy in China. He sighed as his eyes passed over the report about ongoing fund-raising efforts: "Cries of hunger can be heard everywhere; however, before relief efforts have even begun, the threat of more fighting is again on the horizon." There were also numerous missing persons ads: "Have not heard from you, please get in touch with me as soon as you see this."

"Please drop us a line to let us know you saw this notice."
"We've had no news of you since the war last year, please contact us if you see the—"
"I have searched for you in vain in Tianjin and Beijing, anxious as to your whereabouts."
"Miss you much, please let me know where you are currently stationed."
"We heard you were working at some weapons factory, please notify us about how to reach you."

Dr. Sun shivered. He could feel the cold air rising slowly from the floor-boards. He was a strange man in a strange land. When he thought of the North, he envisioned abandoned farms, cracked earth, and troops with fat ponytails who, lying down, periodically puffed from their opium pipes. In the North you were faced with an intricate web of relationships among factions; oftentimes a crisis could be averted simply by throwing of a well-timed birthday banquet. Undeniably, the old powers still had their strong-hold in the North, which was why Dr. Sun had to continue to kowtow to Li Yuanhong. This president of the Republic who took men from every walk of life into his home was a calculating, ambitious strategist. Even his present ploy of stepping out of the limelight did not stop him from wining and dining the governors of Henan and Hubei. Li was using his reputation and seniority to prevent Duan Qirei from putting only his own men in prominent posts once Duan took office.

Dr. Sun put the newspaper down. He was gripped by a sense of power-lessness. What connection did Li Yuanhong and his band of conniving col-laborators really have with the revolution in the South? In the North they were still deeply attached to the old system and the old way of doing things. Although they had donned the cloak of the Republic, whenever talk turned to the old ways of the North, they would let Dr. Sun know in no uncertain terms that he would always be considered an outsider. The truth was that Sun himself knew this too. He was not of noble descent. As a child, he had hardly ever tasted white rice. He had grown up in the rural village of Xiang-shan in Guangdong, and because his family was poor, he had attended school only after he turned ten. After arriving in Honolulu at fourteen, he was suddenly exposed to a predominantly Western style of education. His way of thinking began to be oceans apart from that of the ancient continent. He had never wanted to become a high-level scholar-official by passing through the gates of the orthodox examination system, nor had he been introduced to the subtleties of the Chinese bureaucratic system. For many years of his life he had drifted abroad, from London to New York to San Francisco. . . . In these cities, where overseas Chinese could be found, he had befriended the Hongmen group and often assumed the role of "the big brother" himself. The situation changed abruptly when he was among foreigners. With them he spoke English all the time and conducted himself like a cultured gentleman. To the old forces from the North, however, he had never been the real thing; at most he was only a Westernized country boy who liked to try his hand at the odd farmers' uprising. No! he thought fretfully. He had simply lacked that crucial push at the most critical period. In the end, these men who had little or no respect for him would reap the benefits of his revolution simply by gossiping over their opium beds.

Dr. Sun shut his eyes and remembered that he would now have to change his plans to go to Beijing the next day—just because he had caught this cold while standing at the helm of the ship, he reflected with resentment. What repercussions would this have? How many more misunderstandings would this bring?

Had disaster finally struck? she wondered over and over again all these sleepless nights.

Her premonition told her that a catastrophe was about to occur in this vast land, yet she would be helpless in the face of it.

She became more and more enamored with S's hands, his obedience, and his humility. As the lights dimmed, she resisted sleep. She gazed at the last man in her life with great longing.

Amid the aroma of osmanthus blossoms, she vaguely sensed that this would be her last celebration.

On the veranda in the back garden, she put up a row of crinkly streamers in red and green; she also baked a chiffon cake for S's party. After cutting the cake, they relit the candles, which they did not have the heart to throw away. She put her arm around S's shoulder and tried to teach him the foxtrot.

She used to be quite a dancer, but the needle of her record player kept jumping. These days it was not possible for her to acquire a new one.

The shadow of the two of them leaning into each other flickered on the wall. Gradually, their steps fell in sync with the melody while the needle of the record player continued to dip in the same groove. They did not stop dancing until, in total darkness, the candles on the table had died out. She stood still for a minute and reflected that she had harbored this premonition of doom ever since the founding of the new China.

S said he was going to a very, very cold place.

She held on to his hand; his palms were slightly damp. She reached up to touch his face; his cheeks were hot to the touch.

With some difficulty S told her that he had married a woman from the countryside many years before. They had two girls, Yuyu and Zenzen. He had to go back and take a look. He would be back very soon.

Don't go! If you leave, you will not be able to come back. Once you leave this house, no one can protect you! Her heart cried out, but she could not give voice to any of these feelings. She could hear the roar of trucks driving by her house outside—could it be the changing of the guard? Her mind drifted; she seemed to recall her first meeting with S.

There must be an end to all this, she thought sadly. Darkness was everywhere in this day and age.

The warmth of S's face lingered inside her palm before slowly seeping away through the crack of her fingertips. S tipped his hat to bid her farewell. He did not know what fate had in store for him, but she knew. She knew all her fears would materialize.

Standing before the second floor window, she watched as S walked toward the gate. Suddenly, she was overcome with sorrow. She remembered that the last time she had seen Deng Yanda and Yang Xingfo, it had been adieu forever. That year she had sat in the car agitatedly and watched a comrade walk into Shen Bao Agency to deliver a telex protesting Deng's assassination. Fear had gripped her, fear that the enemy would rip the telex from the comrade's hands. Much later her only memory was of S's lifting his hat to her in the rain. The shiny star on his hat twinkled once before vanishing into the darkness.

After S left, she lay on her huge bed for many nights and watched the sky go gray, then light. Just before daybreak her blood would always freeze and her heart would beat madly for half a second. She thought she saw the knob on her door turn slowly. *S would push open the door and place his warm hands on her waist. He was coming to give her the usual prewake-up rubdown.*

She couldn't fight the tide. Sometimes courage left her. She asked herself, was she going to stand by and simply watch as S walked away? Her eyes had followed him from behind the curtain. It was drizzling and her eyes had turned misty too. Many days later she could still hear the sound of the military jeep revving up in the rain. How ironic! She remembered she had once believed the view put forth by Helen Snow in the journal *Shanghai Women*. Helen had said, "Chinese women appear to be more courageous and honest than Chinese men. Madame Sun being the best case in point!"

More time passed, and then everything stopped at that one second when she heard the news.

First, she learned he had arrived home safely. Then she received news that he had suffered a stroke after drinking. She knew that in her lifetime, she would not see S again.

She began to feel what life was like without S. Every inch of her body where his hand had pressed began to itch and ache. It was as if her bones had suddenly grown sharp teeth and shiny, bright pins were pricking and needling her soft flesh every second of the day.

As a woman of seventy, she was too old. And to start at the beginning again, she was too late. She knew that even if S recovered, she would never see him again. Not because of her age but because she knew the sequence of time. They had no present; therefore, how could there be a future?

Luckily, he still had those two little girls. She was going to try to get them to come to Shanghai. Yuyu and Zenzen were the only family S had left.

For ten consecutive days Dr. Sun's fever raged. He recuperated at the Zhang Yuan Hotel.

The newspapers in the North were filled with speculation about his falling ill in Tianjin. Headlines such as "Purportedly Here Yet Where Is Dr. Sun?" spoke of the gathering suspicion that Sun Yat-sen's coming down with the flu was just a front. Some guessed that Dr. Sun was trying to resolve internal differences in the Nationalist Party between the pro-Communist and the anti-Communist factions. Inherent differences in the party had to be ironed out before he could set foot in the capital. Others wondered whether Dr. Sun's absence was related to the instability of the Guangzhou government. They felt certain that in a show of good faith, he would disband the government. However, many still saw him as an opportunist who was waiting his turn in Tianjin while support for him grew—he would make an appearance only when all parties had given him the green flag. More saw Sun Yat-sen as a conspirator, claiming to head north alone to discuss matters of national importance but secretly harboring ambitions to get his troops to continue their northbound expedition. From the start Sun had never meant to work peacefully alongside Duan Qirei. . . .

These accusations prevailed because no one had seen Dr. Sun's condition. By now his sickly pallor had snuffed out much of his former, much praised revolutionary spirit. He knew very clearly how the numerous failures and life on the road had left its mark on him. No longer was he as hopeful and driven as before. He was never known for reticence and always thrived on a good debate. But after losing his temper at Duan Qirei's representatives that day, he leaned heavily on his cane and was unusually silent as he hobbled back to his room.

As Dr. Sun lay on his bed, he tried to calm his breathing. He knew it was not yet time to admit defeat, but he really didn't have an alternate strategy in place. After learning about Duan's vicious scheme to mislead everyone, he could only issue a lame statement in retaliation. He rubbed his chest as a sudden pain caught him. Duan, the sly devil, had convened the National People's Convention when in reality the politicians and soldiers were deliberating how to divvy up the loot. He had fooled everyone by distorting the main objective of Sun's journey north. Of course, this was only one of the many tricks Duan had up his sleeve. He had made sure that he arrived in Beijing a few days before Dr. Sun's arrival in Tianjin so Duan could quickly set up an interim government. At the inauguration Duan had expressed a willingness to respect all former treaties signed with foreign countries. This was directly in opposition to what Dr. Sun had advocated. The two representatives Duan had sent over had Sun peruse a resolution reached at a cabinet meeting that said all former treaties were to be abided. Dr. Sun was furious about the wording; he lost control and yelled at the envoy: "While I labored to abolish these treaties abroad, you are respecting them in Beijing. What is the logic behind this? If you are only looking for a life of ease; if you are so terrified of these foreigners, why turn around and welcome me?"

Dr. Sun sighed. He sat up in bed and shook the little brass bell on his bedside table. He summoned someone to bring him the telegrams that Duan had sent him the previous month. His temper flared as he reviewed them. One line from a telegram he received just before his departure read, "You are a visionary. Your journey northward and your mission are highly anticipated. You are at the forefront of the North and South reunification." Another telegram that was passed to him from Xu Shiying read, "The commander-in-chief is the one who shapes the revolution and the one whom the people revere. If you do not make a personal appearance in Beijing, nothing will be resolved." At the time Duan even cozied up to the press by pretending he would be party to the alliance only if Dr. Sun made his way north. But look how the tables had turned: when Dr. Sun finally docked in Tianjin, Duan, in an interview with the newspaper, claimed maliciously that "Sun Yat-sen's buffoon-like method of abolishing the treaties cannot be accepted!"

Dr. Sun lay back in bed again. He would be returning home having accomplished nothing, and he would become the subject of ridicule. He had insisted on making this trip north and had informed only a few old comrades of his intent. At the time he had witnessed Cao Kun's demise and saw it as a turning point for the North. He had felt hopeful again.

He had always been too naive—at the outset and subsequently. He had gone to the North twice in the past. The second time he had fallen into Yuan Shikai's trap but what about the first time? Dr. Sun felt dejected just thinking about that experience. It had been 1894, when he was twenty-nine. He had realized that his medical training alone was not going to save the country, so he had naively thought of appealing to Li Hongzhang. At the time he had sought help with the wording from a fellow Cantonese friend, Zheng Kuanyin, and the top scholar Wang Dao. Li Hongzhang was tied up with the battle in Lu Tai and only later sent word to Dr. Sun through a friend of Wang Dao's who was working as a copywriter for Li to "wait until after the war." Sun had felt completely defeated and left for Shanghai very soon thereafter. He had no wish to dredge up this appeal matter from the past. Aside from the humiliation of not being taken seriously, he was embarrassed that he had resorted to the "appeal" method, which smacked of imperial kowtowing. The more he thought about it, the more embarrassed he felt. He wanted to forget it had ever happened. Years later followers of the premier would distort this entire event by implying that Dr. Sun actually had sat face to face with the eighty-year-old Li Fuxiang to discuss issues of national concern. Of course, at that moment this was not something the bedridden Sun could envision.

Sun Yat-sen stared out the window; only a few yellowing leaves still hung on the trees. He knew his goals for coming north would not be realized. It was impossible to persuade those brutal warlords. He suddenly remembered the fierce words he had uttered in Kobe before he left: "If anyone abuses the role of a soldier and stands in the way of fair discussion, I will personally see to it that these people pay a visit to the emperor!" From where he stood that day, he saw the worst signs possible, but was there really still time to turn back? He would return home ill and dejected, but what was another black mark against his name? It would just prove that he was an empty talker who had grossly miscalculated a situation again. He had little political capital left. He didn't know if there would be another chance to stage a comeback.

She began to steadily gain weight at about this time. She changed into the Maoist uniform, slipped her feet into flat shoes, and stood completely inconspicuously next to her comrades for a group photograph.

Everyone was finally the same. Nobody was more equal or less equal than the next person, she thought absently to herself.

The problem was she was still not everyman. She possessed only an abstract understanding of the farmers. The trip to pick cotton in the fields was solely for the purpose of propaganda shots. That was the closest she had come into contact with the people.

"Old witch!" She was vaguely aware that those words were spat out behind her back. When she turned her ahead abruptly, she only saw rows and rows of women steadily picking cotton. Where had the voices come from? Every one of the mouths beneath the bamboo hat could have made the utterance; every one of the faces bronzed by the sun appeared identical.

Except her. She was a fraud.

All over the country the drums of war were beating louder and louder. She knew her position was becoming more and more precarious.

For quite some time her name had not appeared on the lists of those invited to important meetings. Rumors about her secret second marriage abounded. For the first time she realized her status as "widow of Sun Yat-sen" could no longer protect her.

She could drop down in class; she go from being a socialite in the occupied territories to a compassionate member of the intelligentsia. But she could not go further down the ladder, all the way down to the level of the masses.

She could hear the voices lashing out at her very clearly: You narrow-minded class-conscious hag!

Of course, she knew her way of life would bear the brunt of criticism. All the happiness she had enjoyed had been contrary to the teachings of the proletariat.

"Our troops face the sun with their feet firmly planted on the soil and with the hopes of the nation on their backs." She covered her ears and quickly switched off the crazy refrain coming over the central radio station.

Her ears were filled with news of Chairman Mao. Outside the confines of her walls, people walked the streets with banners of Chairman Mao. Framed half-portraits of Chairman Mao hung from every room in her home.

When the demonstrators passed her doors, she could hear a loud commotion outside and noticed the chandeliers swinging wildly from her ceiling. She told herself that she had nothing to fear; she had seen most things in her lifetime. Her legs, however, would shake in disobedience, along with her obese body.

All the arrangements for her trip were in place. Prime Minister Zhou stated that the trip up north was precisely to protect her.

Outside her car window the sky looked gray. She noticed that breakfast stalls no longer dotted the streets. She craned her neck and saw only depressed French parasol trees with banners and slogans strewn across them. She could hardly believe it, but the Shanghai of old was nowhere to be found.

All of a sudden, she heard something hit her car window. The Red Guards sleeping in the streets started to wake up at the sound of an object hitting glass. She shut her eyes tightly in fear. The sound of human voices seemed to charge at her like the rampage of a thousand horses.

19

The date of Dr. Sun's return from Tianjin to the capital city was New Year's Eve 1924. It was a sunny but mild day with a strong gust of wind blowing. Sun Yat-sen's body could no longer stand the toils of traveling, and the train proceeded at a pace that was slower than normal. The railroad authorities had designated special compartments for Dr. Sun. Compartment 308 held sleeping quarters, compartment 212 was the dining area, compartment 101 contained the luggage that was going from Beijing to Shenyang, while compartment 132 carried the luggage that was going from Tianjin to Shanghai. The route that the train was taking passed Zhang Xueliang's territory. Although there was a lot of speculation about the state of Dr. Sun's health at the time, Zhang did not want any mishaps to occur and ordered his troops to take extra care to ensure Dr. Sun's safety. Zhang even saw Dr. Sun off at the platform in Tianjin. During those years Zhang Xueliang looked like a man in his prime. His forehead shone from good health, and there were no telltale signs of his turbulent later life. There was even less indication of the benevolent and devout Christian that he would end up becoming late in his life.

At about three o'clock in the afternoon the train brought Dr. Sun through Zhang's territory, all the way to the outskirts of Beijing. At the time the security of Beijing was still controlled by Feng Yuxiang. In the preceding three months the name of the city's police force had changed three times because of the political situation. On October 23, after Feng's rebellion, the police force was known as the Beijing Nationalist Police Department. On November 1, after a cabinet had been instated, Huang Fu renamed it the National Police Department. On November 24 Duan's administration changed the name yet again, to National Police Headquarters. Regardless of the name, however, the commander-in-chief remained Lu Zhunglin. At the time Lu was Feng's righthand man; according to Lu's memoirs, before Dr. Sun arrived in Beijing, Feng was telephoning the police authorities every day from his retreat in Tiantaishan. Feng repeatedly told Lu that originally Dr. Sun had been invited to the North at his behest, but only one to two months later the tide had turned against them. The Chili faction had been wiped out and the Anhui faction was in power. The significance of welcoming the Nationalists back to Beijing had been lost. Power now rested in the hands of Duan. Duan would have been suspicious if Feng had met up with Dr. Sun. All Feng could do was urge Lu Zhunglin to ensure the safety of Dr. Sun's entourage. Because of these instructions Lu was especially nervous about the crowds at the entrance to the train station. He secretly climbed abroad the train at Yung Ding Gate Station and tried to coax Dr. Sun to avoid the crowds by getting off at Yung Ding Gate.

With his hat in his hand, Lu walked quickly into Dr. Sun's compartment. Dr. Sun saw the shocked expression on Lu's face and knew that he was taken aback by the appearance of the man before him. Perhaps Dr. Sun's frailty could be attributed to his reclining on the bunk rather than sitting on it. What Dr. Sun could not see was how pale and desiccated his complexion seemed. With some effort Dr. Sun shook Lu's hand and exchanged a few pleasantries, but he was insistent about disembarking only at the final stop.

Dr. Sun's guess had been correct. At that time his safety would be guaranteed. At 4:20 in the afternoon his train pulled into the station. A huge crowd had gathered, and one could see the word *Welcome!* written on small white flags as well as an assortment of slogans on banners as Dr. Sun's aides helped him off the train. Dr. Sun was barely able to nod and acknowledge his supporters. He was escorted to his car with his feet almost off the ground. Sitting in his limousine, Dr. Sun could see that the motorcade behind him was dotted with the blue and white Nationalist flags. He could also hear a band trumpeting the notes of a march. From his car window he could see Liyang Gate and the Front Gate. Beijing was a city that was built on geomancy principles, and the central point on the map was the target he vowed one day to overthrow. The last Manchu emperor had long since abdicated, and Fu Yi had been chased out of his palace by Feng's troops. However, Dr. Sun reflected, he had still not managed to realize his dreams. Fourteen years after the Xinhai Revolution, which originated in a remote province of China, he was still without army, money, or outside support aside from Russia. This was why he had to make this trip north. The situation resembled his return to Shanghai in 1911. Rumor had it that he had stashed piles of cash in his luggage; even his comrades harbored secret hopes that this was true. At a press conference Dr. Sun replied that he did not have one cent to his name, but he did bring back the spirit of revolution. What he did not count on was that, many years later, he still had only the spirit of revolution to his name.

With these thoughts on his mind, Dr. Sun tried to appear energetic and waved at his supporters outside the windows. Behind him escorts were busy distributing fliers to people on both sides of the street. The sheets of flapping paper looked like colorful butterflies dancing about wildly in subzero temperatures. All along Changan Street shouts of "Long live Sun Yat-sen!" and "Long live the revolution!" could be heard. Even the shriveled branches on trees in Tiananmen Square bobbed along with the wave of voices. Dr. Sun was surprised by how his comrades had managed to mobilize so much support in so short a time and could not help but think that one of the reasons was that the people here loved him. But he had become less and less vocal about such sentiments. "Most of the citizens in China support me!" Was this really true? In recent years Dr. Sun had given voice to these words on different occasions until he himself could not distinguish whether they were true. In the last ten months he had suddenly arrived at a realization because of the revolution in Russia. He reflected on the past and saw that popular support was precisely what he lacked and what forced him to consort with one or more of the warlords. In other words, Dr. Sun's limitation as a revolutionary lay exactly in his inability to rouse the masses. From the time he had sworn to overthrow the Qing dynasty, he had had to rely on his advocacy, reputation, willpower, and powers of persuasion to get by. Of the lot, his indomitable willpower had exerted the greatest influence. Even when the revolution was riding at its highest, Dr. Sun could stir only the hearts of students, overseas Chinese, and a small batch of soldiers from the South, but stir the hearts of those overseas Chinese he did. With his silver tongue and master salesmanship, he ignited their passion. He had managed to sell them war bonds that would never see maturation. The words "to the value of 10 U.S. dollars—principal and interest of 100 dollars to be collected on V-day" were printed on piece after piece of worthless paper. Like a trickster of the highest form, he had forfeited the trust they placed in him. . . .

The distance from the front gate to the Beijing Hotel was short, yet within those few minutes Dr. Sun had recalled half a lifetime of defeats. Had his revolutionary cause saved China? Or had it wreaked even more damage? The more powerful warlords at the time were busy abusing their centralized authority, while the lesser ones toyed with the administration of the provincial governments. Shamefully, his base in Guangdong was the worst of the lot. In the last year the party had split after he tried to reorganize it. His attempts at straightening out party finances had only drawn criticism from foreign countries and businessmen. More and more people felt that Guangdong was a bad apple that he refused to weed out. Then there was the uproar caused by the local enterprises. The overseas newspaper *China Weekly Review* even went so far as to call him "China's darkest stain." Inside the car Sun Yat-sen suddenly dropped his hand. He felt a hopeless agony wash over him.

The vicious undertones in the recitation of *Quotations from Chairman Mao* and the blaring of the intercom on Tiananmen Square, coupled with the sound of sirens whizzing by, reminded her of the scene of her ailing husband's return to Beijing.

She remembered his final days. He was still gambling on the sentiments of the people who lived on this land. A few years later the sentiments of the people seemed to surge in accordance with his prediction, and good fortune seemed to grace this ill-fated and turbulent land once again. However, she was sure her husband never guessed that popular sentiment would converge in this capital city where Communist propaganda runs rampant.

Inside the car, she wrapped herself tightly with her old coat. Popular sentiment had had the last joke after all, she reflected.

This refurbished building, which once was a prince's residence, had very high ceilings and thick walls. The rooms were massive and mostly empty. She couldn't find a comfortable corner where she could curl up and while away the afternoon.

She was awake for longer and longer spells at night.

In the dark she would recall with regret how she never really knew her husband's sleeping habits even though they were married for ten years.

She had slept so well back then. Put it down to youth. Even when she later came to Beijing to accompany her bed-ridden husband, she fell asleep easily.

During her vigil after his death, however, she was constantly awakened by nightmares. What should she do next? With her eyes wide open in the night, she would tell herself not to cry. But the tears fell quickly. She would sit up to look for a handkerchief and almost hear the melancholic sigh of her husband on his deathbed.

Now, caught in this void of darkness, she really couldn't cry. Wrapped around her were arms of flabby white while the sound of labored breathing escaped her throat.

The longer she stared into space, the more she began to remember, even the most irrelevant things. She remembered meeting the Russian advisers with her husband one year: Marin, Adolph Joffe, General Galen, and M. M. Borodin. She especially remembered the chief adviser Borodin. He had a deep, resonant voice that sounded like a smooth baritone. She liked listening to his unaccented English. Her husband, on the other hand, was more calculating and pragmatic. Even though he kept reiterating the need to look to the Russians as teachers, he took only what China needed. He had never been one who believed overly in ideologies.

What had happened a few years after her husband's death? Russia had begun massive purges. The news came that Adolf Jeffe had committed suicide, Borodin had disappeared, and General Galen had been executed. In Stalin's book of definitions every person was a foreign spy.

Until then she had never really understood. Now she realized that the more idealistic the revolution, the greater the cruelty. Otherwise, why was it always the sons and daughters of the revolution who were devoured first? To a greater or lesser extent, it was because of her that after 1949 they had come to China to live, put down roots, and give to the New China. Yet one by one Rewi Alley, George Hatem, Epstein—all these foreigners who came to China with fervor and passion—were now being defamed.

Were they alive or were they dead? she wondered sadly. It wasn't that she didn't care, but she couldn't even fend for herself now.

She switched off all the lights in her room and drew the curtains tightly. She had too many long, lonely nights to think back on the things she did wrong.

Did she betray her upbringing? Her family? Her class? Whatever the verdict, she had paid with her life and her youth. What more could be asked of her? The problem for them was that her betrayal had not been complete enough. What they wanted from her was betrayal of herself, of her once tender and love-filled heart, she thought.

Was it Lu Xun who said it? She seemed to recall it was Lu Xun who once commented that the most painful thing in life was to be awakened from a dream and realize that in fact there was no way out.

If there was no way out, why wake someone who was fast asleep?

The sky darkened earlier in the North so she would always lie clothed in her big bed at an early hour. For days on end she wished she could just go on sleeping.

Occasionally, she would dream of her husband. After she moved to Beijing, she dreamed of him three times.

In her dreams he was always in a crowd of people. She didn't seem to recognize him. He had changed in some way; the expressions on his face were different. He had never worn an expression of bewilderment. When she woke up, she retraced the dream carefully and wondered whether it had indeed been her husband in the dream. Perhaps she hadn't dreamed of him. She opened her eyes. In the lamplight she saw in front of her only a picture of Chairman Mao. Were her days so bleak that she could no longer remember what her husband looked like anymore?

Her cousin was dead. She had hung herself in a garage. It was the end of the Song family. In her mind the whole of Shanghai was also sinking.

"Taking one's own life is a sin!" she muttered to herself. You cannot die! she told herself.

When she soaked in her tub, she sometimes wished the water would just rise over her head. She thought that if she chose death perhaps it would feel something like water. No matter how coarse and inhospitable the external environment seemed, for one second you felt heat and moisture envelop you.

You cannot die, she warned herself.

It was 1968.

News of the death came from abroad. The deceased was her youngest brother, Zian. Only news bearing such force could cause her heart to ache palpably. Its intensity revealed that she could still feel pain. When it hurt that much, she was reminded of her miscarriage. The pain she felt seemed to come from the deepest recesses of her being and rippled outward.

They were quite a few years apart. Zian had always been the baby of the family. They had not seen each other for many years. She had hardly thought of him, yet she knew she loved him. They never said much to each other and seldom met; perhaps that explained the deep attachment she had for him.

After Zian died, she realized that even the most cherished and tender things in life perish and turn to ash. She didn't know this before. As a young widow, she was completely ignorant. Later, having survived the assassination attempt, she was shaken to her core and furious, but this was different. This time around she was constantly reminded of Zian's face—how perfect it was, like the immortal boys found in Greek mythology.

Death was on her mind in the ensuing days. Strangely enough, it was S's visage, before he had his stroke and the physical sensation of his finger on her skin, that stood between her and death.

Which morning was it? When Dr. Sun woke up at daybreak, he was thoroughly disoriented. His aides vaguely heard him muttering something about Guangzhou, the place that was lost, found, then lost and found again. He was still troubled by the news he had heard the night before. Chen Jiongming had proclaimed himself commander-in-chief and had joined forces with Lin Hu and Fang Binren from Jiangxi to invade Guangzhou again. When Dr. Sun opened his eyes, he thought he saw bellows of cannon fire and gun smoke as well as the rapid muddy waters of the Pearl delta before him. Guangzhou was marked by his failure. When the torrential rains came, white steam would rise from the tarmac and remind him of smog and contagious diseases run rampant. He looked again. The warship that had weathered the good and the bad with him was now a red ball of fire in the eeriness. The sun setting above the swamplike triangle was flecked with blood. He noticed how the streets and alleys of Guangzhou were once again bathed in red, with frightened women trying to duck into trenches as dirty-looking soldiers hounded them as if they were prey. Was this the outcome of his revolution? Broken tiles and splintered beams were scattered everywhere. Even the Yuexiou Building, which was supposed to be the best lookout onto the river, was now a burned-out skeletal structure. Dr. Sun wanted to get as far away from this city as possible. Whenever Dr. Sun returned to Guangzhou after his period of exile, he never felt the joy of homecoming as the ship docked at port; rather, he felt like he was returning to a trap. Some people constantly urged, "Let the Cantonese run Guangdong" or advocated the construction of a "New Guangdong." When he needed to deploy troops there, some worried that the outside troops could mean the end of that province. Why could they not comprehend the notion of one land, one entire country? For people like Chen Jiongming, a unified China was too big. Thinking of the traitor's name cleared his head. He rubbed his eyes and spat in contempt. I'm not dead yet so let him dream on. . . .

The truth was that Sun Yat-sen had never guessed that Chen Jiongming would stoop so low. Not only did he ruin Sun's plans to go north, he had even thought about assassinating Sun. It was the worst kind of example for comrades-in-arms. For Dr. Sun, who placed a strong emphasis on intraparty ethics, Chen's betrayal was a direct affront. It angered Sun further that he had actually placed his trust in Chen once upon a time and had regarded him as a loyal follower. After defeating Yuan Shikai, Dr. Sun should have understood the importance of having your own forces behind you. Instead, he had sent telegrams to all provinces to declare a cease-fire as soon as Yuan was dead. Not long after, Dr. Sun also ordered the Zhunghua Revolution Army, which he had put together, to disband and go home. The result was the evaporation of the little military power he had accrued after defeating Yuan. Later, when the military government chased him out of Guangzhou, the only arsenal he could rely on was Chen's. On the other hand, Dr. Sun had never liked dabbling in military power. He was far happier talking about his ideals and persuading by arguing his beliefs and principles. If need be, he would fall back on the strong bonds of friendship that existed between him and his comrades. However, at critical times none of that mattered. He was always one army short. This was his downfall. Not only did he not have an army, he was inexperienced in the art of war, which explained why he could never read a situation correctly. At the start of the siege against Yuan, Dr. Sun had announced that with two infantry divisions he could confront Yuan directly. At the time Tan Renfeng had rudely interrupted him to ask where he thought the two infantry divisions would come from. By the way, how many people constitute two infantry divisions? What could they accomplish? Dr. Sun, in truth, had never given these implications serious thought.

Dr. Sun turned on his side. He stared at his bony, frail hands that clearly had not experienced manual labor. He was reminded again of how out of place he looked in the attire of commander-in-chief, with white gloves on his hands and a top hat perched on his head. Even though in name Sun Yat-sen was the leader of the revolution, the only chance he had to "command" the forces at war was at Chengnan Gate. Surrounded by the thunderous sound of canons, he presided over his fighting comrades. He remembered seeing Huang Xing's shiny face amid the shelling; Dr. Sun sensed how adrenaline must have been coursing through Huang's veins. Dr. Sun walked a few steps behind the firing cannons and felt the uncontrollable shaking of his calves. His second chance came in 1918. This time around he put on his commander-in-chief garb and sat at the helm of the ship that was bombing bases on land. It was during the military government period, and the warlord Mo Rongxing had behaved with blatant disregard of Sun's existence. Mo had had the audacity to execute people he had captured from the commander-in-chief's headquarters. Dr. Sun was furious and ordered the warships *Tungan* and *Yuchang* to bomb Mo's bases. When the commander of one of the warships showed signs of hesitation, Dr. Sun stood up and instructed the naval officers to fire immediately. Because he had had a modern education, Dr. Sun had always felt more at home commanding the navy than the army. Later, when Chen Jiongming betrayed him, only a few naval vessels continued to pledge their allegiance to Sun. Some faction or other was always trying to bribe officers to turn their backs on him. Dr. Sun had witnessed too many betrayals during his lifetime; he could count the truly loyal followers with one hand. In his mind only Zhu Zhixing, Deng Jian, Xu Zhungchi, and Chiang Kai-shek qualified. Of them, Zhu and Deng were already dead—and what about the men before them? In Dr. Sun's drowsy state, Huang Xing's chiseled and courageous face emerged in his mind again.

He seemed to hear Huang Xing's steady voice reminding him gently, "Sir, you represent the Republic but not the circle of power." But could one actually separate the Republic from the circle of power and the military powers behind that circle? Ultimately, he had learned to rely on guns—a valuable lesson he had learned from the politics that exhausted him. Yet when you finally understand what is more important, you need to also give something up to obtain it. Dr. Sun remembered the inauguration ceremony at Whampoa Military Academy when he had personally handed over the academy seal. His mind turned to the man who was even more impatient than he was—Chiang Kai-shek. Dr. Sun had never seen someone wear a soldier's uniform more impeccably. Nonetheless, he was still anxious for Chiang.

Perhaps Dr. Sun's somewhat blunted political instincts had seen the future of these young men who claimed to be his followers. He seemed to be able to foresee how his so-called rightful successor later would use political events to rid himself of the older comrades and embark on a political feud with Sun's widow that lasted many years. Chiang even used the protection of Madame Sun as an excuse to send his political enemy to his death, and then Chiang stopped the scandal from leaking out. Of course, what Dr. Sun could not envision was his wife's choosing to side with one faction in the future. But controversies aside, he needed to focus on the present. Dr. Sun wanted more than anything to lead China out of the darkness surrounding it. His repeated failures had made him see his own shortcomings. More and more clearly, he saw his revolution going nowhere. External factors aside, he was far too mild mannered to be a revolutionary. He knew this all too well. In just about all acts of revolution, the person who dares to do what others do not emerges victorious in the end.

22

She had always known she was one of the lucky few. Having endured and witnessed great upheaval, she had somehow managed to survive.

The men in her life—the ones she loved and the ones who loved her—had all disappeared into the silence. She had outlived them all.

At long last the Cultural Revolution seemed to come to an end. She felt that a part of her had died long before that.

Physically, she was dying. Bit by bit, her lifeblood left her, yet she was still waiting to die. She never knew that death could be drawn out like a stick of toffee.

In comparison, her husband's dying within three months seemed too fast. As the saying goes, "The brave die once while the coward dies a thousand times." The fate that befell those who managed to fool death was to see how all dreams eventually turn to dust. So, ultimately, who was braver? Was it she or her husband?

One night she had a nightmare. She was kneeling on the floor, and across from her, also kneeling, was her younger sister, Meiling. They were leaning toward each other, eyes locked in battle like two vicious dogs. They stared at each other in anger, eyeball to eyeball.

Whose side fired the machine gun?

Dead or alive?

Why don't you look for cover?

Even after she woke up, she found it hard to catch her breath. It was a replay of the tragic scene she had witnessed in Guangzhou all those years before. Her heart pounded from the fear.

A few days later she received news of the death of her brother-in-law Chiang Kai-shek.

From a photograph sent to her from abroad, she immediately saw how the light in Meiling's eyes had started to fade.

As expected, Chiang Ching-kuo assumed power after his father's death. She knew that even if her sister did not go abroad, her role on the other side of the straits would be limited.

The more she thought about it, the more ludicrous it seemed. From now on the two sisters would compete to see who could live the longest.

She calmly listened to news of Mao's death. As a precautionary measure, she changed into a black satin pantsuit. She was born in the same year as Mao and both of them had enjoyed the occasional cigarette. In the earlier years she had even cautioned him to cut back.

Not long after that, she heard news of Jiang Qing's arrest. She had known ever since Mao's death that this would be Jiang Qing's inevitable fate.

Who were the future victors? Obviously, those who had endured all and were still unperturbed and silent to the end. It was an easy guess.

Post apocalypse, she felt lucky just to be alive. All she could think about was how she could take care of her old friends.

There was S, who was now paralyzed in a home. How old was he now? She was afraid to think of the answer. She could accept her own downward spiral, but to her S always remained at one point in time—the night they said good-bye. Only then could she always be the object of affection of a thirty-year-old man.

She thought this was a good time to determine the whereabouts of those two girls.

23

In room 506 of the Beijing Hotel, Dr. Sun refused to receive visitors, issue statements, or attend any social engagements. For the first time in his life, he became the good patient. He was still attentive to outside changes, but no heartening news was forthcoming from Canton. Tan Yenkai's army had retreated from Jiangxi to the borders of Canton; Chen Jiongming's ally Fang Binren in turn invaded Jiangxi, while elsewhere things were at a standstill. What troubled Dr. Sun was the imminent postwar conference. He was concerned not only about its provisions but also that Duan Qirei had chosen the day before Dr. Sun's departure from Tianjin to alert all parties involved that February 1 would be the date of the conference.

Dr. Sun had trouble sleeping. He struggled to decide whether his party should attend this conference, which would be monopolized by Duan. The following morning Wang Jingwei stood by Dr. Sun's bedside and waited for his verbal instruction. First Dr. Sun made a few introductory remarks, noting that he had come to Beijing to speak his mind but prolonged illness had delayed his doing so and meant he had to write down his views because the postwar conference would start soon. Then Sun wrote down two conditions. He hoped that in addition to the military officials whom Duan had invited to the conference, businesses, student associations, business associations, and farmers' associations would be allowed to participate as well in nongovernmental capacities. The second condition was that issues pertaining to military structure and fiscal spending should be decided by the People's Congress, which was to be convened at a later date. He felt he was actually making a huge concession. When Wang sealed the document with a small stamp with Sun Yat-sen's name on it, Dr. Sun looked away. He felt he had been reduced to groveling.

His gaze settled on Wang as he tidied up Sun's brushes and ink stone on the table. Wang wrote beautiful calligraphy and had the most open and friendly face. Here was a man who did not harbor any ulterior motives. Compared with Sun's gambling nature, which could change at whim, Wang was just a learned and talented scholar who was subject to melancholic mood swings. Although tales of his assassination of the regent were widely known, Wang wasn't by any means a bloodthirsty and reckless fellow. Dr. Sun knew Wang was given to bouts of depression. During the second revolution he had written the lines of a poem that read,

> My heart hesitates to climb the stairs,
> For fear of seeing a sick kingdom.

Later in Japan, when Dr. Sun recruited comrades to join in the cause, Wang had to continue his exile abroad. He often wrote of his yearning for the beauty of Jiangnan in March and his hankering for women. Dr. Sun did not share his sentimentality, nor did he have room for nostalgia. He believed Wang was truly devoted to him, not simply because of the seventeen-year age gap between them but because psychologically Wang needed to look up to a strong leader.

After Wang left the room, Dr. Sun began to deliberate on the future of his comrades and the Nationalist Party. He believed his health would improve soon, but this monthlong hiatus in bed had made him realize that he really wanted to bow out of politics, at least for the time being. What weighed on his mind was who could replace him. In the past year the problem had become more unsolvable. The left and right wings of the party had still not reconciled, so no one within the party could take his place. Even when he was the party leader, he had had to resort on numerous occasions to leveraging his personal connections to prevent spats from escalating uncontrollably. He had told Zhou Lu when he reorganized the Nationalist Party that the spirit of the revolution lay in the strong emotional bonds between comrades. But probably closer to the truth was that all the emotional bonds had rested with one person in particular. Dr. Sun stared at the cane that rested next to his bedstead. The gold knob glistened brightly. After so many trials and tribulations, he fully understood the importance of leadership. When the second revolution had failed, Dr. Sun knew it was because of the lack of solidarity within the party. He had been only a puppet leader. When the China Revolutionary Party was established, he had insisted on the importance of obeying orders. He stipulated that all party members had to take orders from him without reservation or question. Party members had to be sworn in before him and have their fingerprints taken. At the time Huang Xing was strongly opposed to the whole process, believing it to be hugely discriminating. He felt insulted that they were being treated like criminals. Dr. Sun, however, had never questioned the validity of these rules. Dr. Sun regarded his mission as historical. He always made sure his photograph was on every registration card, and he signed his name, stroke by stroke, on every single document. Ironically, because Sun Yat-sen now stood for the party and the party for Sun Yat-sen, the question of his successor became almost impossible to resolve.

Dr. Sun thought of the comrades who had been closest to him in the last couple of years. In terms of seniority Hu Hanming was rightfully his successor. But Hanming was becoming an embittered old man who had no handle on the art of politics. In terms of ability Liao Zhongkai was one of his top men. He had a ferretlike visage and small beady eyes, but he had many sound ideas. His wife, He Xiangning, was well respected and liked. During the United League period everyone called her "the queen" and her home was often filled with visitors. The problem was that Liao Zhongkai was staunch in his beliefs. He was severely criticized for his handling of the canton's fiscal problems, and his bid to reorganize the Nationalist Party had met with much dissent, to the point that he had become a target for the right wing. Dr. Sun had to exercise caution when he looked at the bigger picture.

Right then he remembered his old comrade Yo Lie. He was Dr. Sun's former classmate, along with Yang He-ling and Chen Shaobai. In the old days they often met at the Yangs' ancestral home to talk about their dreams of revolution. People called them "the Four Robbers." After the Republic was founded, Dr. Sun hardly saw these friends from his youth. Perhaps just as well because Yang He-ling, who was one year younger than he, exploited his association with Dr. Sun wherever he went. In a letter to Dr. Sun he even had the audacity to write, "Since I was there with you right from the beginning, I should rightfully be there when the benefits are reaped." The harsh winter landscape outside Dr. Sun's window brought many dormant memories to life. Memories of his childhood village mingled with flashes of violent pain. He longed to walk on the little path next to his home once again. He wished he could jump wholeheartedly into the cool stream in the village. In the heat of high summer he relished the feeling of reeds tickling his neck and the light on the water blinding his vision. After a few dives he would splay out his arms and float quietly on the water. . . . He wasn't aware how much time his reverie had taken, but he sensed an unseen shadow was hovering over him. Dr. Sun so wanted to return to his past, to walk in the classroom he had studied in when he was ten, to gaze at the marks on the stone floor, to listen to the old villagers talk of long-haired robbers, to touch the saplings he had planted with his own hands. If he could only walk along the fields back to the crumbling temple and straighten the statues he had wrecked all those years ago. Then he could etch every forgotten detail into his memory. Thoughts of the past mellowed him. In his mind the faces of his old friends grew clearer and clearer. Chen Shaobai now held a position in a bank, and Yang He-ling was serving as a special correspondent in Hong Kong. At that instant Dr. Sun was sorely tempted to invite Yo Lie to head the party. Why not? Yo had the advantage of not being affiliated with any particular faction, and he had been there right at the beginning. If you retraced the family tree, you would see that before the United League there was the Revive China Society, and the beginning of the Revive China Society was the start of everything. Once upon a time these ideas of lineage, history, and tradition had seemed feudalistic to him, yet now they crackled and sparkled like wildfire in his mind.

When he awoke from a dream again, a corner of his blanket was damp. He had no idea where the drops of sweat on his forehead had come from.

The Shi Ca Hai Lake started to freeze over, and she knew she would be able to hear the sound of blocks of ice pushing against each other if she stood on Yin Ding Bridge.

She had always wondered what color the lake would be if the ice started to melt. Would it be gray or blue? Would you be able to see the dark shadow of branches from trees reflected on the water?

What kind of trees did they have in the North? She could be certain only that they were not French parasol trees. She constantly thought of her home in Shanghai. That white building on Xiafei Road with the magnificent backyard and emerald lawn. She had never cared for the traditional Chinese style of architecture, where artificial hills and pools were part of the planned landscape.

She really detested this dank and dark residence she lived in—eighty years of her life in exchange for imprisonment. This place in this northern city held no happy memories for her.

Many years before, her husband had died here. Now, was it her turn? It wasn't even possible for her to die in a place of her own choosing.

She sadly acknowledged that she would not be returning to the South.

Doctors had instructed that she was not to venture outdoors, let alone to embark on a long-distance trip. The South and all its fond memories were lost to her forever. She remembered that at around this time of year a soft drizzle would always grace the South.

In the end, the true victor was always time.

She reminisced how time, so silent and imperceptible, had turned her into an old, clumsy woman. Staring at the itchy red rash that had suddenly materialized on her forearm, she understood how time grants the lucky few longevity, only to steal everything away from them little by little. Your memory, your mobility, even your dignity to live fall away. She thought about heaving her heavy frame up, but the thought alone tired her. Her only wish was for someone to come along with a cool balm to sooth her discomfort.

Sometimes she woke up crying. Tears streamed down the side of her cheeks. Had she been weeping in her sleep?

She woke up from dreaming only to become that dried-eyed old woman again.

In her dreams she often thought about S's feet. At the bottom of his one sole were frostbite scars. S had slim, elegant toes. When he walked around her home in Shanghai wearing those plastic slippers, the pallor of his feet resembled pale moonlight that had been spilled over the bridge of his feet.

So many years had gone by, interspersed by a Cultural Revolution. . . .

She came to understand how much S had had to endure. In her dreams she forgot how immobilized she had become; instead, she knelt down for the first time and gently massaged his feet the same way he had massaged hers so many times before.

She had another dream in which the shutters in her bathroom were drawn. A sensual atmosphere pervaded the bathroom. There was a tub full of warm water and S was busy scrubbing her back. She let her entire body fall forward in relaxation. When the water started to cool, S suddenly stood up with his back to her. In the dream she remembered a pale green birthmark, the size of a palm, conspicuous against his pale white buttocks.

When she woke up, she felt dazed. She called the people in Shanghai and instructed them to raise S's rank again. She wanted to be sure that he would be treated like the highest official at the sanitarium.

25

According to Ma Xiang's recollection, for a few days before January 20, Dr. Sun's condition had been quite stable.

Lying in bed, Dr. Sun's diminishing eyesight sought signs of life outside his window. Everything was blanketed in gray; winter in Beijing was devoid of green. In the dim light he seemed to see the voluptuous curve of mountains. At the foot of the mountain mangoes and star fruit lay strewn across the ground. He knew he was seeing Sun Mei's farm on Maoyi Island. Thinking of his older brother evoked in Sun a sense of dismay. In the early days he was constantly asking Sun Mei for money. Each time he would walk off with tens of thousands of dollars from him. When the Republic was newly founded, people had nominated Sun Mei to serve as governor of Guangdong, but Sun had been opposed to the idea. Sun Mei had come to Nanjing to reason with him but didn't get very far. Four years later his brother had died. Dr. Sun had never given much thought to his family. Other than refurbishing their ancestral home, he had done very little for them. In truth, Dr. Sun had given even less thought to himself; moneywise, he barely had a cent to his name.

Turning over, he gazed at his wife, who was hunched over his blanket, asleep. She was probably exhausted from the night watch; at that moment she appeared so serene. He wanted to lean over and brush back a lock of hair that had fallen between her eyebrows, but he was too weak to lift his arm. He gazed at her fair countenance; she had lost a lot of weight lately. In the dim light she appeared strangely exotic. He knew many of his old comrades were opposed to his marriage because of the huge age difference between them. Hu Hanming, Wang Jingwei, Zhu Zhixing, and Liao Zhongkai had all spoken against it. On several occasions, to seal their mouths for good, Dr. Sun had been forced to hide behind words such as, "I am human, not God," and "You have the liberty of seeking pleasure outside but I don't."

Now that he was lying sick in bed, he was sure people were blaming the sexual needs of a young wife. They were wrong about her. She had never been particularly sexual, perhaps because she was worried about harming his health, but he also sensed a deliberate suppression. Did this suppression cause her cheeks to flush and the skin around the corner of her eyes to turn a faint pink in sleep? When she was naked, she always acted so docile and pliable, as if she were a virgin. Her nipples were still small flowers in bud and, aside from the smell of clean soap, they held no taste when one sucked hard on them. He often felt the need to prove himself to her. He labored to find a spot she would find pleasurable and loved to hear the faint moans of a woman when she was close to orgasm.

In his eyes she always seemed composed and elegant. Either her upbringing or her education at Wesleyan College for Women in Macon, Georgia, had taught her to hold herself slightly apart at all times. He remembered how she would read English books aloud to him. In winter, when the fireplace roared and crackled, her soft southern accent would fill him with joy. The two years that they spent at No. 29 Moliere Street in the French section were probably the quietest of his life. The books he had written were rejected by publishers on the ground that the government forbade freedom of speech, so he had to use his own money and persuaded Huacheng Publishing House to print his books. Nonetheless, the time he spent working at home was a time of relative ease. The house they were living in was a gift from an overseas Chinese sympathizer, and their needs were simple. Occasionally, when they had visitors, they would go to a small neighborhood Fuzhou restaurant. If Tang Shao-yi came to the house, they would just order a fat salted duck to add to their daily fare. When their old friend Wu Ting-fang came to play chess, he would always take his leave just before dinner so they wouldn't need to feed him. Although Dr. Sun did not have a car back then, he would hire a horse-drawn carriage for long distances without giving safety a second thought. Who would trouble with a man who had so obviously fallen out of power? He liked to take a stroll with his wife to the bookshops; sometimes they would go to one on Sichuan Road, other times they would walk to Qipan Street on Fuzhou Road. He had ordered a shipping almanac printed in England from the bookstore and learned a great deal about things like tonnage and ship draft.

Although they had limited means, in retrospect the time he had spent in that apartment in the French section was wonderfully regular and predictable. Every morning he would eat a bowl of steamed swallow's nest, and after lunch he would have some stewed apple. The ulcers that had plagued him for many years began to heal. At night his favorite activity was to spread the map of China out on the table and circle the canals, ports, and railways in red and green ink. When the clock struck nine, his wife would see his two nephews to bed. The father of the two little boys had died, and the two boys were staying with Dr. Sun for the time being. Sometimes, when he watched his wife bending over to make their beds, he felt he could live like this forever. But deep down he knew he couldn't lie to himself. Even though he was said to be in hibernation, not a day went by when he didn't pay close attention to developments between the North and South. At the time the president in the North was Xu Shichang, and in the South his representative was Hu Hanming. Hu had urged Congress to exercise its authority at Sun's request. Thus the peace settlement talks between the two sides were doomed to fail right at the onset. On the other side the Hebei and Guangxi factions were eyeing each other, while Sun Yat-sen was secretly in contact with the Anhui faction led by Duan Qirei.

It was one of the few instances where he played the political game. In order to foster closer ties with Duan, Dr. Sun and his wife traveled to Hungzhou on the pretext that they were touring the West Lake. Lu Yongxiang, who was a general in Shanghai under Duan's faction, served as go-between and at the most scenic spot in West Lake informed Sun that Duan was willing to back Sun's return to Guangdong. With that guarantee in place, he was able to later return to Guangdong and assume the position of president. In the end, however, no amount of planning could predetermine the future. That scoundrel Chen Jiongming curtailed his plans, and the sly and cunning Duan made a fool out of Sun.

Thinking back, his one regret was that he had missed the beautiful scenery of West Lake because his mind had been so consumed by politics. It had been a rare opportunity for him and his wife to travel to a popular destination. Try as he might, he could recall only that she had carried a white parasol because she was afraid of getting sunburned on the shores of the lake. Her fear probably stemmed from the skin condition that had plagued her for many years. As for the rest, he couldn't remember a thing. During his lifetime he had neglected many women who worked alongside him. He was either too busy devising a scheme or he was in the midst of executing something else. His whole being was absorbed in brokering for peace between comrades or expanding his influence on land. Sometimes he would blame himself for his negligence but never for long. He always believed time was on his side and he could make up for it later. Did that ring true? At that moment he remembered a poem that had been recited at their wedding:

> You like spring, I like autumn.
> Should you take a step forward and I a step back,
> We'd be in the heat of summer.

How could humans possibly delay the seasons? Dr. Sun pondered dryly. From autumn he had stepped into the winter of his life, while his wife was about to enter her summer. Here was a woman eagerly awaiting the rains of July. With sadness he looked at her dewy complexion and refused to believe that he would leave her for good just when she needed a man more than ever.

Looking back on her life, she believed her dalliance in politics had been a wasted effort.

The left and right wings now meant little to her. All roads seemed to lead nowhere. The various revisionist ideologies that people talked about were filled with despicable lies. She was overwhelmed by a staggering sense of futility.

The electric fans weren't working in her Beijing residence. She sought refuge in the porcelain bathtub again.

She suddenly recalled in the earlier years how her husband had a bush of graying hair around his crotch. She realized that with age, hair from every part of your body actually changed color.

She looked at the area beneath her own pelvic bone. It was covered with a dove-gray mat of hair that could ignite no desire. She felt utter disgust for her bloated, oversized body.

Sitting in the water, she reflected sadly that her body no longer held any female attributes other than her shrunken organs. Love had been the mantra of her life, yet what vessel did that love now exist in?

In her memory, of course—now she remembered. The beginnings of a dazzling smile began to appear at the corners of her mouth. She knew for certain that inside her memories love was alive and kicking.

At that moment a kind of light appeared on her ravaged face. A bright, clear light still burned in those eyes that had witnessed countless disasters. It was almost as if a dust-free world had materialized before her, and the image transported her past the years of hardship across to the shore on the other side. . . .

That world was clean.

The male world where power struggles reigned was inevitably filled with the smell of blood. She, on the other hand, had never hurt anyone intentionally. Her hands were free of blood.

Past mid-January, Beijing's weather started to change. There wasn't a cloud in the sky and the air was cold and dry. As Dr. Sun stared at the ceiling, his breath felt hot and the area around his tongue tasted bitter.

As his fever subsided, he was able to slowly turn over onto his side. A distinct smell permeated the room. Was it the smell of disinfectant or was it the rich perfume of flowers? In the next instant the smell of wet moldy uniforms filled his nostrils. He reflected on his past defeats and humiliations and wondered whether later generations would laugh at his stupidity. His emotions fluctuated as wildly as his body temperature. Had he misjudged the views of the populace? When the old regime had collapsed, he had believed the power of this great land was ready to be unleashed and his blueprint for the new republic could be realized. And why not? Even in his current state he still believed that the tide of democracy was too strong to be stemmed; the people were on his side. His problem was a simple one: at critical moments he had lacked the necessary clout. He felt wide awake and immensely confident in his political instincts. He had an ear to the heart of the nation and, with a little more time, he would be able to leverage the power of the revolution onto his ideology again. The strengths of his precepts lay in their comprehensiveness. His agenda for a political society would be three-pronged: nationalism for the people, sovereignty for the people, and livelihood for the people. These three dogmas covered all possible scenarios for China in the future. However, at the same time many people were still in the dark about his cause. Sun suddenly felt despair wash over him. Did he believe talk of principle and ideology could ultimately enlighten the masses? Other than principle and ideology, what did he have to offer? He had a meager troop of loyal soldiers, thirty thousand at most, and could never stand up to the warlords from the North. Yet, in order to fight the impossible fight, the Supplies Board was doing all it could to amass funds. Warlords, big and small, already seized taxes from the people so the government had to resort to legalizing and then taxing the opium trade and gambling dens. His coffers were so empty that he had had to publicly advocate the need to legalize gambling!

Dr. Sun's mind whirled as he looked for words to defend himself. His breathing became labored. How could he feed the troops if he didn't start selling government property? If he hadn't legalized gambling, how would the soldiers have been able to go north? Although the heat pipes in the room were working, judging from the clanking noises, he could still feel the cold seeping in from the floorboards. The icy wind pricked his joints like a thousand tiny needles. His teeth started to chatter loudly. He remembered that when he heard how enemy troops had destroyed Guangzhou, he was so incensed that he banged his head against the wall as his subordinates looked on.

Later that day his old friend Wu Jinhuan arrived at the Beijing Hotel to see him. Wu had been invited to Beijing by the Qing Palace Review Committee to inspect the treasures of the palace. He was staying near the Beijing Hotel and would often stop by to visit Dr. Sun. As Wu sat by Dr. Sun's bedside, he heard him mutter a string of unrelated phrases: "Find it hard to unify China" . . . "Guangzhou is a losing battle." . . . "Zhang Zuo-lin was never serious about cooperating." . . . "Chen Jiongming, you can't expect me to simply discard the revolution." Wu gazed at Dr. Sun's feverish face and decided they could wait no longer. They had to follow the doctor's instructions and prepare a stretcher to take him to Xiehe Hospital, which was one street away from Wang Fu Jin Road.

Pomegranates, bauhinias, osmanthus, crab apples, roses, and clumps of plum blossoms began to sprout in the garden of her Beijing residence. Orders came from the top that ten years of hard times were finally over, and the gardeners should arrange the pots of evergreen Nippon lilies into the Chinese character for longevity in her honor.

She did not want anyone to pull up the blinds in her room, which faced the garden. She was accustomed to the darkness and how the perfume bottles on her bureau glistened ambivalently and mocked her.

All her best years were hidden under a cloud of stale scent.

She remembered when she was a little girl. Dressed in her velvet pinafore and woolen bobby socks, she looked just like a doll as she stood at a leafy street corner in the occupied territories.

She remembered hearing the sound of a passing carriage. She grabbed her papa's hand tightly and jumped into the carriage. As usual, Papa's hands were soft and warm, and he always took her to safe and wonderful places.

Her mind took her further back. She recalled the house where she had lived as a child on Yuhang Street in Hongkou, Shanghai.

Redwood furniture lined the four walls of the house, and an ornately carved bed was placed in her parents' upstairs bedroom. Downstairs, in the Westernized living room, there was a piano, and beyond that room was a small Chinese sitting room. Three bathrooms were spread out between the two floors, and the most bewitching bathroom was the one in her mother's bedroom. Had the bathtub been aqua colored? She remembered when Mama sat in it; a pale green steam would rise magically from the sides.

Song Qingling could never resist creeping silently up the stairs and sneaking a few peeks through the half-closed doorway before running away.

Unfortunately, she will never be able to go back eighty years to the days when everything was perfect.

They were six siblings. Three boys and three girls. Their home was always filled with the sound of music and laughter. How she loved holding her baby sister in her arms. Meiling was born chubby and round, and when Song Qingling fell on the bed because Meiling was too heavy to hold, the little angel would giggle hysterically with no hint of pain.

Later Song Qingling recalled the river that ran next to a nearby street. Fields of golden rapeseed flowers grew on its banks. She remembered how the water would trickle gently past a window and the bamboo rods with laundry hanging from them. The clothes were freshly washed, with water still dripping from them.

She was already a junior high school student then. For her spring vacation she visited the countryside with a few classmates. When she stood on the steps leading up to a stone bridge, a thought came into her head that made her blush: Wouldn't it be nice if she could find a handsome young boy with whom she could see eye to eye and wash his clothes for him for the rest of her life?

She was never given the chance. When she turned fifteen, she went to the United States. Her English was always better than her Chinese. For the daughters of the Song family, even if they did find a man they saw eye to eye with, fate did not grant them the luxury to be ordinary.

Papa once gave her a necklace. Unlike her other sisters, she rarely had the chance to wear jewelry. The gold heart-shaped pendant with vinelike engravings on it became her only adornment.

Even though so many years had lapsed, some nights she would still take out the pendant from her bureau and hold it against her cheek. She imagined the touch of her father's thick hands patting her face and how with one swoop he would lift her onto his head.

Why did Papa choose a solid heart rather than a gold cross for her pendant? She thought she could understand why. Even Papa's motivation in printing Bibles had been to earn money for the revolution. Throughout his life his cause had been a worldly one—to save an ailing country from disaster and to take care of his six children, who were born in Shanghai.

In the end, his all-too-sharp intuition had molded the destinies of his children and China.

Next to her face the heart-shaped pendant felt just like her Papa's big hands, freezing when he had just come in from the cold but warm and comforting in a matter of seconds. She had always known that of her five brothers and sisters, she had been Papa's favorite.

A part of her childhood remained particularly vague. Sometimes she could not be sure if her thoughts were memories or just a dream.

She remembered Papa's escorting her out of the foreign concession areas into the Cheng Huang Temple to watch the Lantern Festival. She was wearing a short maroon coat with a shiny brooch attached to her collar. She remembered that brooches were considered exotic and Westernized back then and were seldom seen. The closer they got to Yu Yuan, the more crowded the roads became. It was impossible for the carriage to get by so, they got off to walk. She held on tightly to Papa's hands but suddenly she felt her brooch slide off. Worried that people were going to trample it with their big feet, she released Papa's hand to pick up the brooch. When she lifted her head again, she was surrounded by unfamiliar faces. Where was Papa? He was already lost in the crowds. Her entire body turned cold from fright.

A long time seemed to pass before Papa's big hand found her again. Only then did she start to cry out loud.

Later her relationship with her family went sour to the point that she was forced to leave home.

She forsook her papa for Dr. Sun and betrayed that most intimate father-daughter trust.

Probably at her mother's urging, she received her dowry after her wedding. A double bed, a closet with drawers, a satin blanket with a hundred little colorful boys on it, and a hand-embroidered bridal dress . . . everything she would need was there. This demonstrated the sophisticated side of her mother's upbringing: you can harbor anger, but you must never forget your manners and at all times remember to keep up appearances.

She could never forget her papa's grief-stricken look or, more to the point perhaps, nothing could disguise how much she had hurt her father, despite his years of experience in compromise.

She had let go of his hand only momentarily in the crowds, but before she knew it, she was surrounded by strangers. Where was Papa? She hadn't held onto his hand tight enough.

"Did that momentary lapse of the hand signal the beginning of a lifetime of turbulence?" she thought to herself.

At three o'clock on the afternoon of January 26, the stretcher bearing Dr. Sun arrived at Xiehe Hospital.

According to the next day's newspapers, "Dr. Sun's temperature flared as he was admitted into the hospital. The diagnosis was that he was in a critical condition and had to undergo surgery right away."

The files of the Nationalist Party show that Dr. Sun went into surgery at six o'clock that same afternoon. According to the *Founding Father Chronicle*, "Upon examination of the liver, it was clear to the naked eye that cirrhosis had completely set in and liver cancer had progressed to the point that surgery would be in vain. That evening, three surgeons from Germany, Russia, and the United States took specimens from three different sections of the liver for testing. Thereafter the surgeons washed and stitched up the area. Results from a microscopic inspection diagnosed Dr. Sun as being in the final stages of liver cancer. The long-term causes of the illness could be traced back to ten years ago and the immediate causes to two to three years ago. Dr. Sun's condition was not curable and too late for radiation therapy. The doctors concurred there was very little Western medicine could do for him."

On February 5 an article entitled "Sun Yat-sen's Postsurgical Condition" documented the situation in the operating theater in great detail. "The point of incision was to the left of his body. The incision was five inches in length. As regional anesthesia and arterial clamps had been administered, Dr. Sun did not feel any pain and bleeding was minimal. After the incision was made, a strawlike instrument was used to extricate the pus from the liver. The pus was deposited on a wad of gauze in a dish and taken to the laboratories for further examination. After extricating the pus, the doctors cleaned the infected area. The doctors found a malignant tumor known as liver carcinoma. The outcome of the laboratory analysis showed that Dr. Sun's cancer been dormant for more than ten years. During the fifth year of the Republic, Dr. Sun had suffered from ulcers, which were caused by the liver cancer. On the evening of the 26th, Dr. Sun's condition was still precarious postsurgery."

Her corpulence had immobilized her to the point that she could not bend over. She was imprisoned within the thick walls of the residence; yet if she strained and leaned over, she could still smell the bottom of her perfume bottles. The residual scent lingered ghostlike in the air.

She knew that the scent came not from traces of perfume at the bottom of the bottle but rather from fragments of memory from her former life.

Sometimes she would recall the smell of her husband's hair cream on his pillowcase. No matter how hard one washed the pillowcases, the smell stayed.

With that familiar scent her thoughts drifted back to her girlhood. In 1913 she had run into Sun Wen (Sun Yat-sen) for the first time on the streets of Tokyo. As she stood next to her older sister, Ailing, she looked at this man who was almost thirty years her senior. For many years she had heard stories about him, and even when they met he had been hiding as an exile in Japan. She noticed a strand of his greasy hair that had fallen onto his lapel. Instinctively, she felt like leaning over her sister to brush it back for him.

Dr. Sun was a close friend of her father's, and at the time Ailing was working as Dr. Sun's secretary. As they stood near the home of Akiyama Sadasuke, Song Qingling dodged a rickshaw that had darted out of the alley. She had just returned from America and found the back alleys of Tokyo too narrow. The man in front of her took off his hat, and she inhaled the scent of his hair cream; it was a sticky yet strangely fresh smell. An absurd idea suddenly came to her. If she were to tidy up this man's appearance for him, she would have to claim him for herself.

After a few days she went with her sister to Dr. Sun's home in Akasaka. A plaque hanging outside his door said "Nakayama," which was the Japanese alias he was using. At the entrance was a wooden stairway that led straight to the second floor, where Dr. Sun lived. When they entered, he wasn't there. Inside they found a small bed, a wooden table, and three worn chairs. Dr. Sun had probably left in a hurry because the remnants of what seemed like lunch—two plates of sushi—were on the table. A half-read book lay next to it. She took in the details of the room. It was clearly a bachelor's room.

When she thought about it later, she remembered that it had been raining that day. Looking out his window, she saw a graying cotton kimono hanging on the wash line, sodden. At the head of the bed was a paper umbrella. She smiled in spite of herself when she saw it. Sun Yat-sen had been reduced to the life of a pauper because of his cause against Yuan Shi-kai, but just a year before this man had been the president of a country! Who took care of him now? Crinkling up her nose, she seemed to smell that omnipresent hair oil again amid the wet, dank air.

She was very different from her sister. Her older sister was level-headed and always counting the odds. She knew her older sister was a competent secretary but one who never truly believed in Dr. Sun.

She, on the other hand, really enjoyed hearing Dr. Sun speak. His earnest yet excited tone of voice tried hard to contain the urgency that was about to bubble over. It was the kind of urgency that believed the world could still change.

When she sat across from him, she noticed his well-oiled sideburns were slightly curled at the ends. She yearned to touch this man of fifty, who had a stormy past and who had presided over a nation. She imagined herself leaning over and caressing the ends of his hair the way she would scratch behind a cat's ears.

What she liked best was to listen to him speak as she sat in the audience. He had the ability to capture a crowd. At those times she felt feelings of tenderness wash over her. She even felt proud that she was this man's friend . . . or was it girlfriend? Well, at least his best friend's daughter. On stage Dr. Sun's every gesture had a powerful impact. "The welfare of the people," "the survival or destruction of China"—she liked these resonant words that transported her to another time and place. Sitting on the wooden bench, she felt as if she were hearing the somber toll of bells back at Wesleyan.

Dr. Sun's concluding words were, "Let us set our hearts on saving China. By so doing, China would become a strong country that can stand side by side with other great nations of the world." As she sat in the audience, she felt that she shared this vision and that the vision would be realized very soon. Greatly moved, she got up from her seat and applauded with both hands.

How young she had been then!

She had been accustomed to wearing little round hats and lace-edged dresses. In Japan, during their hasty wedding at Umeya Shokichi's home, she also wore a hat.

Hats always reminded her of brides. When she was studying in the United States, the ribbons that trailed behind a classmate's wide-brimmed hat seemed like the train of a wedding dress to her.

Thinking back, their wedding had been a slap-dash affair. Even now she regretted that the single most important ceremony of her life was devoid of the blessings of her parents and friends. Even the night before her wedding, Madame Umeya was still trying her best to dissuade Dr. Sun, telling him that "if you marry Miss Song, who is young enough to be your daughter, it will take years off your life."

That same evening she wrote a letter to her sister Meiling and her brother Ziwen explaining their elopement. "I am willing to sacrifice everything, do anything in the name of Sun Wen."

Was it a girlish passion that made her write down those words? Or was it a kind of patriotism? Or was it mere foolhardiness mingled with a sense of higher purpose? Too many years had gone by, she sighed. She could no longer remember.

Outside the operating room comrades were alarmed by the terrible news. On the evening of the operation Wang Jingwei sent a nationwide telegram urging "all comrades to return quickly" to Beijing. To the core members of the Nationalist Party who would have to take over in the future, the most pressing issue was not how they could reposition themselves but rather how they were going to accommodate the immediate problems facing them.

At midnight that evening the Nationalist Party Central Committee held an emergency meeting at Hu Tong's ad-hoc office. This committee had originally been established and chaired by Sun Yat-sen in Guangzhou. Because Hu Hanming and Liao Zhongkai were still in Guangzhou, and Shao Yuanzhong was in Shanghai, Yu Yoren, Wu Jinhuan, Li Dachao, Chen Yoren, and Li Yiyin, all comrades from Beijing, were asked to attend the conference.

A strong sense of gloom pervaded the meeting. After several hours of debating whether Dr. Sun should be told his diagnosis, whether his diagnosis should be publicly announced, and whether he should be asked to make a will designating a successor in advance, they could not reach a conclusion. Wang Jingwei, who was presiding over the meeting, found it hard to focus. He seemed to be in a state of sacred anticipation. He was praying for a miracle. After making some preliminary remarks, he spent the remaining time wiping tears from his eyes.

When dawn was about to break, the people in the smoke-filled room felt depleted and tired. Wang Jingwei stood on the podium and made a few concluding remarks:

Comrades, Dr. Sun has always been extremely resilient. He is more robust than the average person. Even if he cannot fully recover, I am sure he will be able to extend his life by another one to two years. For the time being, let's keep this news from him. We do not want to upset him unduly. Let's wait until it is absolutely critical.

Wang Jingwei promised the comrades he would ask Dr. Sun's doctors to tell him when Dr. Sun's condition became critical, so he could ask Dr. Sun to make a will.

She actually did recall the night of their wedding. Dressed in a Japanese *yukata* bathrobe, Dr. Sun suddenly looked half a head shorter than he did in the daytime. He also appeared older: the skin around his collar sagged, and the moles and liver spots on his face stood out.

She was somewhat taken aback and wondered whether her decision had been too hasty. Sun Wen was now truly her husband. She had traveled here all the way from Shanghai to sign their marriage contract. Aside from her parents' opposition, everything had gone according to her wishes. She should be content, yet she remembered her sense of panic when the contract was signed. This is it. . . .

Changing into her nightgown before the mirror that night, she had a good look at herself. She looked like a flower at the height of her beauty; her red lips were plump and full. She hesitated for a minute—her classmates in Georgia were still being courted by boys at sorority dances, while here she was, giving her hand over to a man of fifty.

Many years would pass, and only after she had met S did she fully understand how Sun Yat-sen's heroic image had tipped the scale in his favor. Otherwise, the age gap should have given her pause.

She remembered how people on her husband's side of the family always appeared to be older than they were. Even her husband's child seemed older than other people of the same age. The first time she saw her husband's only son at the house on Huanlong Road in Shanghai, she noticed how avuncular he looked, even though he was only one year older than she. Her face felt flushed. What was he supposed to call her? Was he to call her "Mom" or "Auntie"? Luckily, he left before he had to call her anything. When she thought about it later, she couldn't help but laugh. How was it possible for a girl of twenty-three to have such an old-looking son?

Even though so many years had passed, she still often dreamed of Sun's thin lips moving in speech. He had a hypnotic hold over her. In those days, when she was at her most impressionable, she believed anything that her husband uttered.

Her own lips were full and plump, some would even go as far as to say thick. She knew that meant she was a sentimentalist.

She discovered after their marriage that Dr. Sun was a very good teacher, but outside his role as revolutionary-mentor, her husband was a little coarse, impatient, and even absent-minded. When it came to the big decisions, he sometimes found it hard to make up his mind.

During the years they lived in Shanghai, her husband would often give talks to comrades, journalists, and foreign guests in their living room. Sometimes she really wanted to pull up a small stool and sit by his side as he spoke. But more often than not, they were asking the same old questions. The warlords of the North, the warlords of the Southwest, the brutal warlords, warlords who were violating agreements, warlords who were occupying territories, each trying to dupe the next. . . . Standing in the shadows, watching her husband's troubled face, and seeing his lips move so fast that his message was devoid of intonation, she suddenly felt lost. All her emotions were tied to this one man. Yet being a politician, his mind was mostly on the staccato revolution. Her sensitive heart, buoyed by the tenderness of giving up her virginity, longed to latch on to him . . . but why did she feel so hollow at times?

She came to understand Sun Yat-sen's notion of women only after becoming his wife. When a group of overseas Chinese revolutionaries spoke about women from their past, it was very much in an off-hand manner. There was no mention of love as love obviously had no place in a man's domain. As to what happened to these women or what went on in their minds . . . that had never been within the men's scope of concern.

When they saw her, they tactfully kept quiet. Guarded, they looked at her as if she were a foreign creature, not quite sure what to make of her. She had heard about her husband's various romances. In her mind they were not so much romances as flings. Even when she heard the stories, she pretended not to care—not to demonstrate how generous she was, she consoled herself, but because she believed that a one-night stand by definition was rushed, superficial, and forgettable. It showed only how easy it was for men.

Never had she wanted that kind of love. In her memories she chose to believe her relationship with her husband was special, unlike the relationships he had with other women. Once, not long after they were married, she came across a letter he had written to his mentor, Cantlie. The words read, "My wife was educated in an American college. Not only is she the best assistant one can ask for, she is also my friend."

Reading these words, she should have been glad, but she was filled with inexplicable disappointment. He viewed her differently only because of her background. In her husband's eyes she was just another woman.

When she had proposed to elope, Sun Wen had been taken aback. Obviously, it was something he didn't think a woman would have suggested.

She sighed: in the end he was still unable to step into her mysterious and unbridled inner world.

33

He felt as if he were coming back from a very long dream. He struggled to open his very heavy eyelids. First, he saw the leafy shadow of a plant, then the blurred image of some glass tiles. He recalled that he had been admitted into a hospital.

The anesthesia dulled his senses; he could feel his incision stinging slightly. In his semidetached state he heard a loud crack, as if icicles were breaking against the windowpane. It was probably the sound of steam popping in the heat pipes—he noticed wisps of white smoke evaporating in the air.

He could hear a muffled sound from an adjacent room—very likely the guards were changing shift. He didn't have the energy to say anything. When the distant winds began to howl in the background, he fell asleep again.

34

She lit a cigarette as she continued to sit still. Her eyes fell on the newly framed photographs on the wall. She felt as if she were looking at another era. Back then, did she love this man? How long ago it all seemed. Nonetheless, she was certain she would never come across another person like Sun Wen, who harbored so many dreams to make the world a better place.

Not only did he want to pinpoint the exact position of canals and beaches, he also wanted to build 200,000 miles of railway in a space of ten years. He wanted to study everything from the way salt crystallized to how coal was mined, right down to how food was canned.

"It is my hope to develop this harbor in the limited time available so that it can be on the same scale as New York."

Sitting on the bed, she recalled her one visit to the harbor on Qinghuang Island in the North. It was the first part of Dr. Sun's National Construction Plan. During her visit the cold wind blew furiously. The landscape was bare and desolate. "Where was the harbor?" she grimaced. Dr. Sun's naive words flew in the wind like pieces of incense paper.

She knew his grand plans would not be realized. She had always known her husband had too many unrealistic dreams, but she understood that his earnest desire was for China to become strong. "Therefore,—" she had sat in front of her desk and written down those words as her husband dictated the outline of his plan to her.

The tip of the cigarette between her fingers glowed like starlight in the darkness. Bits and pieces of the past, the difficult years, came back to her. During the spring of 1918 the weather in Guangzhou was humid and damp.

Her skin had developed a rash. From her window she noticed a white film of vapor rising from the Pearl River. When she shut her eyes, she seemed to smell the decay of animals on the surface of the water.

Who could have imagined that within a few days they would be so bad off that they could not even pay for their daily expenses? She watched the somber look on her husband's face and knew that the dreams brought about by the Russian Revolution in October had disintegrated. She remembered when news of the Russians' success had reached Guangzhou, she had compared the Russian leader Lenin to her husband and found Sun Yat-sen to be every bit as qualified. Like Sun, Lenin had returned from abroad in time for the armed uprising, but Sun Yat-sen had been a revolutionary a whole six years earlier than Lenin. In retrospect, however, it seemed as if those six years were entirely wasted; they were now stuck in a dead end in Guangzhou. Her husband had miscalculated once again, believing that Guangzhou would serve them well in both an offensive and defensive situation. On the face of it, he was the commander-in-chief of the military government, but the truth was that they were at the mercy of the warlords, and there was no conceivable way out.

She still vaguely remembered her husband's decision to attack Hunan from Guangxi. Was that the first Northern Expedition by the Nationalist Party? She wasn't sure.

In December of that same year she had accompanied her husband to his headquarters in Guilin. She had never seen a more chaotic province. On the side of the roads were bungalows with curtained entrances and the words *Interrogation Booth* written on them. Step inside, and you found a den of people smoking opium in broad daylight. Soldiers openly ran casinos. Guilin was filled with troops of every faction, and at any time one soldier would walk into a brothel and cause a fight to break out. Each morning the abandoned corpses of soldiers were found at the foot of the city's walls.

She could hardly believe what she was seeing. She had always known that her husband was a dreamer, but only at the front lines did she realize how far he would go, the kind of crap he had to take, in the name of these dreams.

Sometimes, in her more terrifying nightmares, she would recall the manner in which she had escaped from Yueixiu Lo. Amid imminent danger, she had been disguised with Captain Yao's straw hat and her husband's raincoat. In front of her, her husband's troops had charged out of the building while looters tried to storm the front door. Her vision had blurred and sweat poured from her face. The enemy was firing at them from the bridge near the presidential office.

She heard the rebels scream, "Kill Sun Wen! Kill Sun Wen!" She had cursed Chen Jiongming for his brutality but drew comfort from knowing that Dr. Sun had already given them the slip.

After they had crossed the bridge, she experienced shelling again. She couldn't walk another inch, and the guards had to drag her by the shoulder, one on each side. A bizarre sight suddenly greeted her. Two men, facing each other, were squatting on the floor of the alley. They stared at each other unblinkingly. She realized that they were dead—probably killed by the onslaught of bullets. She had screamed and felt her stomach contract in pain. In her dreams she would always peer down and see blood oozing out of her lower body.

Many years later, when she thought back on the child she had lost during Chen's coup, she would always feel a strange sensation in her body.

She had accidentally come across pictures of an unborn fetus in a book. The huge head was grossly disproportionate to the shriveled thin body. The fetus attached itself to the uterus and grew bigger with every passing day.

She could still feel a bundle of blurred life in her body. But she could also feel the taste of blood burning at the back of her throat. Her stomach would heave from the metallic taste.

Some people welcomed news of Dr. Sun's failing health. Zhang Zuolin publicly stated that with Sun Yat-sen out the way, the path to unification would be smoother. This wasn't the first time that Dr. Sun had been seen as an obstacle to unification. In 1922, when Xu Shichang resigned as president of the North, many tried to force Dr. Sun to step down as president of the South. But Dr. Sun refused to give up his position to the likes of Li Yuanhong. Critics, including Cai Yuanpei, accused Dr. Sun of impeding unification. Even the U.S. consul general stationed in China at the time publicly called him "the most obvious obstacle to unification."

Three days after the operation Dr. Sun's temperature and heart rate had stabilized. There was no sign of inflammation. In the twilight his first impression upon regaining consciousness was that the procedure had gone well and he was on the road to recovery. Through the window he could see the building across the road. Judging from its height and his knowledge of the area, he estimated he was on the third floor of his building. From his window he could see the outline of one pagoda tree and four cypress trees. Dr. Sun guessed there was probably a nice courtyard somewhere in the hospital and perhaps a greenhouse too. In one corner of his room was a pot of pink hibiscus flowers. He found himself in a very Westernized setting. The decor in his room had a distinct European flair; the lampshades on the wall had fancy gilt edges that reminded him of his home in Xianshan County, Guangzhou. Dr. Sun had personally drawn up the renovation blueprints for that house. He designed the arch on the veranda that was symmetrical on both floors and adopted an architectural style that was a blend of East and West.

Eyes closed, Sun recalled the two calligraphy scrolls he had commissioned for the house: "Though barely a room, this is my cozy home in Guangzhou." He had been proud of these lines when he wrote them and to this day the words still rang true. When he opened his eyes again, a plane was passing over the hospital and he could hear the whir of the engine. He had presided over the christening ceremony for an aircraft in the past. When he remembered the sound of the champagne bottle smashing against the propeller, he almost sat up in bed. He had christened the first plane made in China as *Rosamund,* after his wife.

The white-on-blue emblem of the flag was painted on the four wings of the biplane while the wheels were a royal blue. It was exhilarating to watch the plane take to the skies right away, flying higher and higher. The trial flight took place at Guangzhou Airport, and Dr. Sun could still recall peoples' joy and excitement as the champagne sprayed across the wings of the aircraft. The plane's taking off symbolized an ascent to the skies as well as the shaking off of poverty and war. It also meant China was flying into the arms of the outside world. But what was happening in the outside world? If the operation had gone smoothly, would he be discharged very soon? As a revolutionary, Dr. Sun knew he was not easily defeated. Even in the most difficult of circumstances, he liked to picture the future with optimism. He often seemed keener about the things happening on the outside than any present danger. Thinking about it, it was probably the same for those foreigners who had come to China. During the war-torn period, a group of international adventurers had arrived at his base in Guangzhou. To them, Guangzhou still held the appeal of revolution. As the painkillers in his body began to wear off, he thought about the air force he had been determined to build. An American air force pilot named Albert from San Francisco had come to his aid. Dr. Sun not only had him training new recruits but soon promoted this young officer in his twenties to lieutenant colonel.

What was the outcome of his surgery? Instinctively, Sun Yat-sen felt uneasy. He tried to turn his head. A scene from the plane christening came back to him. He remembered that Albert had been sitting in the cockpit with Rosamund to his left. When the plane took off, Dr. Sun, who was on the ground, struggled to keep his top hat down and wondered for a split second what would happen if the plane crashed. His wife had only just turned thirty. Ever since they had decided to stay together despite the opposition to their marriage, they had speculated about how they would depart this world. Together they had experienced an assassination on a train platform three years before. A bullet had penetrated the stomach of the chief of staff from Guangzhou, Deng Jian. With his death the planned agreement between Sun Yat-sen and Chen Jiongming had fallen to pieces. Thirteen years earlier, at the ticket booth at a train station, someone had killed Song Jiaoren, who was serving as the interim director of the Nationalist Party at the time. The bullet had landed next to his heart. Although Sun wasn't there himself, he had learned from onlookers that Chen Qimei had howled in anger, vowing that the assassins would not live this down. Sun Yat-sen could imagine the scene. Because of that blood bath a declaration of war against Yuan became unavoidable. In 1916 Chen Qimei himself was assassinated in Shanghai, taking a bullet in the head. As Dr. Sun contemplated the outcome of his surgery, the faces of these deceased comrades emerged before him. One by one, Lu Haudong, Shi Jianru, Yang Zhuyun . . . had all fallen. His mind swirled with the images of their faces just before they died. Compared with them, he had seldom been in the direct line of fire. In the past few years, for security reasons, one to two soldiers well versed in martial arts followed him wherever he went. He had always imagined dying in the arms of the woman he loved while his body was covered in blood; the image was simply too romantic to resist. Yet at that split second when the plane took off, it suddenly occurred to him that he had never wondered what would happen if she died first.

In 1921, amid the sound of cannons firing, he had really thought their time had come. He envisioned holding her hand and breathing their last on the warship *Yong Feng*. As they dodged the sound of cannons in the darkness, Dr. Sun thought of never being able to return to Yue Hsiu Lo. The two of them would float out to sea as outcast lovers. But even under those perilous conditions, when his troops had been reduced to a few isolated warships that could not dock and traitors were everywhere on land, he did not lose heart. In those two months his activities on the ship were limited to studying maps and avoiding torpedoes and the intermittent firing of cannons. Occasionally, when a journalist from an English newspaper came on board, Dr. Sun had to do his best to stifle the profound bitterness in his heart. Thirty years of hard work had been destroyed in a fortnight. During their escape his wife had lost their baby. At the time he had been too preoccupied to dwell on it, while she had remained silent out of respect for him.

The effect of the anesthesia had started to wear off; he could feel the sharp pain again. It seemed to be at the old area just below his stomach, but he couldn't be sure. He knew the success rate for the procedure was low; he couldn't lie to himself. He might not have a chance to tell his wife how sorry he felt about his behavior toward her. His throat tightened as he contemplated the many ways he had overlooked her all these years. Many times, especially when he felt downtrodden and lost, he knew his only salvation was love. The sad truth, however, was that he had never been in love. At that moment upon waking, he touched the still-warm blanket where his wife had pressed her face. She had probably been by his side the entire night. He suddenly remembered that she liked to eat a particular kind of cheese that was flavored and moldy. He also remembered that every now and then she suffered from a bout of eczema that ran in her family. . . . The ties that existed between husband and wife still tugged at his heartstrings. For the first time he felt sorrow and regret toward his young wife. How could he leave her behind?

The pain began to intensify, and before long he was bathed in cold sweat. Feeling the premonition of death, he started seeing images of Moscow in a dreamlike state. In the mazelike imperialist city many grand Stalinesque buildings were under construction. His widow had become hopelessly lost. In a small pub with a fountain in the courtyard, she had fallen drunk. "Madame Sun," someone called out to her and shook her shoulder. Who was it? The voice seemed to come from a very remote place. At that moment Sun Yat-sen deeply regretted that he was not leaving his wife anything, not even a little child. When they were on the run, she had lost the only baby she had ever conceived. As a man of sixty, how could he not know its impact? Sadness would trail his wife all the days of her life. Whenever the soft rain of spring fell, her maternal instincts would be awakened again in her body. The faint acidic sensation would haunt her like a hollowness that was hard to pinpoint. Ever since that time on the warship, he had come to realize that the hollowness would be exclusively hers, not only because death would ultimately separate them but because the wife of a revolutionary had to learn to live with repression. She had never once mentioned the miscarriage. Sun wondered whether his wife would remember that her body had carried a child or would she think, in retrospect, that the bleeding in the midst of gunshots and bullets been merely an illusion?

36

She stood in the hospital corridor, unable to believe that everything would be coming to an end so soon.

She had never thought her destiny would be decided by a man. She had always believed that a woman of free will could enjoy autonomy, even in marriage. Only as her husband's death became imminent did she begin to understand the power play that existed between two individuals of different ages and backgrounds. Her husband's death was an extension of that power play.

She hated the meaningless details of the funeral: the paper wreaths, the tearless weeping, funeral scrolls all over the room, and the repeated expressions of "our sincere condolences" ringing next to her ear. Instinctively, she rebelled against the sisal cloth that spoke of deterioration and bad omen. In her heart she longed to spit at this kind of formality the way she could when she was a child.

In the middle of the auditorium people were bowing to show their respects. The master of ceremonies was reciting eulogies in a loud voice. Was that her husband in the casket? To her it was only a corpse soaked gray in formaldehyde. She really didn't want to be standing so close to the cold, impersonal bier.

The huge coffin reminded her of the ancient custom of burying the spouse alive alongside the deceased; she felt a shiver run through her. In front of her Dr. Sun's former comrades lined up in rows. They had tried to stop him from marrying her and even blamed Sun Wen's early death to some extent on her. She felt they looked at her with a degree of hostility.

Stuck in the cold, morbid air of the funeral home, she longed to return home to Shanghai. But she knew that the sons and daughters of politicians have no home, so to speak. Papa, who loved her above all else, had passed away too. Even on his deathbed Papa had not forgotten the hurt she had caused him, and he felt horribly betrayed by his own friend. Her mother, who came from a well-to-do family, continued to fixate on how she could protect the Song and Ni family businesses. As for Song Qingling's capable older sister, Ailing, she knew in her heart that they would end up in opposing camps one day.

Dr. Sun was kept in the dark about everything, including the announcement released by the hospital to the press. Once a day Wang Jingwei would selectively report on local developments, and Chen Yoren was responsible for the compiling and reporting of international news to him. Chen's report never went on for more than ten minutes at a time.

That day Sun's fever had abated slightly, and he managed to fall sound asleep early that morning. When he opened his eyes, he saw his son standing by the side of his bed. Sun Ke had just returned to Guangzhou on business when the comrades had summoned him back to Beijing.

"You're here?" he acknowledged lamely. He closed his eyes for a moment, not sure of what to say. Sun Ke looked so much like his mother. The older he became, the more uncanny the resemblance, especially when he frowned. Sun Yat-sen was reminded of his ex-wife's expression when she was angry. Sun Ke had obviously inherited his mother's stubborn temperament as well. Dr. Sun grew irritated when he recalled that his son had provoked the feuding among the older comrades and the second generation of comrades in Guangzhou, and he had spoken out openly against Dr. Sun's befriending of the Russians.

Actually, he had nothing of great importance to say to his son. The phrase he cited most often when he wrote to his son was "do not idle away your time," or he counseled his son to read more serious books. Sun Ke enjoyed reading literary works that had nothing to do with the way of the world. Sun Yat-sen could not understand the merit in the likes of Shakespeare. Dr. Sun had become so accustomed to talking about high and lofty ideals in his letters that he was suddenly at a loss as to how he should address his son in person.

As he turned his face away, he thought of his oldest child, his daughter, who had looked so much like him. He had always favored Jinyuan. Jinyuan suffered from kidney failure when she was eighteen. They never managed to see each other again after she fell ill in Macao. She had been dead for more than ten years, but he still felt a dull ache when his thoughts turned to her. Dr. Sun's life as a revolutionary had been fraught with hardship, so he had very few memories of his sons and daughter. In the short two months he had served as the ad-hoc president in Nanjing, he had taken his three children hunting in Zijinshan once. In retrospect that was one of the few happy memories he had of his family. The next year, when news of Jinyuan's death reached him, he had been grief-stricken but not to the point of paralysis. He was always ready to forge ahead with his plans for the revolution. Since their divorce he had given his first wife very little thought. She was a chapter from the past that had faded into history. Strangely enough, this instant, as his son stood before him, he was reminded of the black knit pantsuit that his first wife, Lu, always wore. The yarn had grown more threadbare with every washing until the breeze would blow right through it. Perhaps because Sun was seldom at home in the earlier years, Lu had always been very careful with money. She had raised their three children by herself, and even when times got better, she was accustomed to saving every cent. She was constantly consumed by the small mundane affairs of the day, often bickering about the petty change that servants returned to her after a trip to the market. But she had committed no ill against him; he had been the one who was adamant about marrying someone else. Sun closed his eyes as he relived her desperation when he had insisted on a divorce.

Part of his regret toward their son stemmed from the fact that Sun Yat-sen's in-laws had also suddenly materialized. The chief of the central bank, Song Ziwen, had rushed to Dr. Sun's bedside as soon as he received the urgent telegram from Beijing. Another even more important person was his brother-in-law Kong Xiangxi. He had become the designated representative of the Sun family and was busy receiving and dispatching visitors all the time. When Sun was awake, he would peek at his round-faced, affluent brother-in-law through semiclosed eyes. Kong was rather plain looking, but he had been the man that Song Ailing had chosen for a husband.

Remembering that, he couldn't help but feel the need to size Kong up. In the early years, before Dr. Sun had met the younger sister, Ailing had served as his personal secretary. When they were alone, he often harbored romantic thoughts about her. He had always been careful about concealing his feelings because he felt she was someone who was very much his equal. With her, he behaved like an experienced hunter, relying on instinct. Even when the prey was in sight, he still paused before pulling the trigger. Ailing was incredibly shrewd and had obviously inherited her father's intelligence, but she seemed to lack the benevolent idealism of her father, Charlie Song. After meeting Qingling, he was glad he had not been the one who had married Ailing. Ironically, though, Ailing was probably celebrating that she had not chosen him, Sun Wen thought to himself. At least, she was not destined to become a widow early in life.

His mind in confusion, Sun suddenly remembered that twenty years before he had, on the spur of the moment, asked a random fortune-teller in Chinatown to tell him something about his life. The old man had asked for his birth date and with one hand had calculated that, based on the five elements, Dr. Sun had too much wood in his life, a moderate dose of fire, and too little gold in his fate, all of would ultimately prove detrimental to his health. For some reason Sun had remembered the diagnosis about his clashing five elements. The old man had glanced at him and declared that he would possess some wealth, but if the opposite sex did not get to him first, battle fire sure would. At the time Sun was a tired revolutionary who had walked from one street to the next in Chinatown while pedestrians passed him by. Although he heard the fortune-teller's prediction, he had laughed it off. How could he believe a blabbering old man? What was more, the brothers from Hong Men had sent all sorts of women his way during those early rogue days. In the small motels on the outskirts of Chinatown, he had bedded woman after woman before leaving them early the second morning to hurry on to his next destination. Not only had he cast his wife in the country to the wind, he couldn't even remember the face of the woman he had been with the night before. All he carried with him was the lingering warmth of the sheets. During those days on the road he had quite an appetite for women. He felt virility was a demonstration of masculinity. It was exciting to be so powerful! He remembered the South Pacific, where there were fragrant banana leaves in the room and the animal-like grunting evaporated into the hot air. Sun Yat-sen was sucked in by these memories. . . . To future generations, it seemed unfortunate that these colorful memories were not recorded in the annals of history. The official records of the Nationalist Party make scant mention of Dr. Sun's involvement with and assistance from groups like Hung Men and other secret sects. Instead, there is a self-righteous description that "collaboration existed only on the basis of upholding the Republic and safeguarding human rights." An examination into the nature of the relationship was deemed more suitable for a book documenting the history of these sects. The history of the Republic also contains no record whatsoever of the bohemian side of Dr. Sun's life. Even a novelist had to contend with his holier-than-thou image when it came to describing the real life of Sun Yat-sen. This can be seen from the lyrics of the "National Father Song," which is sung each year in schools when people observe Sun Yat-sen Memorial Day: "Oh, our National Father, you led the revolution and shed your blood."

Later that afternoon Sun took a few sedatives before he turned in for the night. In the next room Sun Ke wrote a telegram to the headquarters in Guangzhou that read: "Arrived in Beijing today. Met Sun Wen. In good spirits. Appeared clear-eyed, rosy and well. Appetite and energy picking up. Temperature this morning was 37 degrees, breathing 24, pulse 100. Best condition since admission."

She recalled that in the 1920s, her sisters were already the belles of high society in Shanghai. Her younger sister, Meiling, with her long bangs, chandelier earrings, and print dresses was the talk of the town, while her older sister, Madame Kong Ailing, was rumored to have buttons made out of diamonds for her dresses.

Madame Sun, on the other hand, was widowed. Her hair was always done up in a tight bun and she wore plain *qi pao*.

She remembered the impression that she had left on foreign journalists: "Since Joan of Arc, countries have aspired to create saints like Madame Sun."

It seemed to be their destiny. Whenever she was down in the doldrums, her two sisters would be having the time of their life.

In 1927 her political journey had come to an abrupt halt. The Wuhan government was in shambles and she was forced to return to Shanghai. In Shanghai her younger sister, Meiling, had just fallen happily in love with her political opponent.

Song Qingling had never blamed her sister. Her younger sister was spoiled and listened only to Ailing. Ever since they were little, she remembered hearing Meiling say, "Sis, you decide, don't ask me."

She was a meticulous collector. After so many years she still kept the article about Rayna Prohme that an American friend of Song Qingling's had written. She placed the article in front of her and put her glasses on to read it. Song Qingling could recall Rayna Prohme's funeral as if it were taking place right before her.

The car lent to Madame Sun by the Soviet Union Foreign Ministry tailed behind the crowds. I tried to persuade her to return to her car; at least it was warmer inside, but she refused. On foot, she circled the city while her beautiful face focused intently on her hands, which were crossed against her heart. Her face was pale from a recent illness. Although a heavy mist shrouded everything that day, I discovered that the exiled Madame Sun was still the loneliest person there. She followed behind the casket of her dearest friend and tremblingly passed through the darkness that had fallen too soon.

She had not brought sufficient clothing or money. Her good friend Rayna had been the editor-in-chief of a U.S. magazine and had accompanied Qingling secretly by ship from Shanghai to Helsinki, where they boarded a train to Moscow. Somehow Rayna had contracted meningitis in China and passed away not long after they had arrived in Moscow.

Song Qingling had been caught in a bind; it was virtually impossible for her to remain in Shanghai. Because her younger sister's love affair with Chiang Kai-shek had become public, rumors of Qingling's reaching a compromise with the rightist government were rife. She was forced to leave.

Moscow was covered in ice. She read about her younger sister's sensational Shanghai wedding. Her family, her relatives, her friends, even the reverend and fellow churchgoers she had known as a child had all been present at the wedding.

She was truly alone now, she thought to herself. Her entire family was standing on the other side of the line. The newspaper mentioned that in the center of the wedding hall hung a picture of Sun Yat-sen. The newlyweds had bowed to the photograph of the deceased premier. Above the photograph were two crisscrossed red, white, and blue Nationalist flags.

In later years she often saw the paintings of ballerinas in different art museums in Europe. The strange thing was that she noticed not only their floating tutus and elegant gestures but also their tired bodies, swollen ankles, and fragile waists. She thought she heard the faint notes of a cello playing in the background and the shadow of death reflecting on the floor.

Suddenly, the white tutus changed into circles of light. She saw the principal ballerina of the Moscow Opera House on stage. Listening to Tchaikovsky's concerto in the background, she had a sense that life, like light, was flickering. During her exile years she could forget all her troubles because no one knew who she was. As they sat on the seats covered in red velvet, her shoulder almost touched Deng Yanda's shoulder.

After the ballet they would always stop by the Metropol Hotel for a drink. This luxurious hotel, which had witnessed the Bolshevik Revolution, once served as Lenin's headquarters. It was still crowded with the rich and the beautiful. Many elegant socialites clad in fur sat behind its tables. In comparison, her black *qi pao* made her look dowdy and worn.

On the dance floor people danced to the strains of a violin. She leaned against Deng's broad shoulders and thought how this man symbolized the epitome of romance to her. His romanticism even manifested itself in his political beliefs. Deng had served as the dean of education at Whampoa Military Academy as well as minister of agriculture. More recently, he had deviated from his leftist inclinations and devoted himself to "the third way." Basically, he disagreed with both sides of the equation and on principle would never side with the ruling party.

Thinking back, the time in Moscow was actually the happiest of her life. They were similar in age, and both had been forced to live overseas by the people in power. All this, coupled with a sense that theirs was a meeting of true minds, drew them to each other.

"Aren't you afraid?" she had asked Deng. She had witnessed too many bloody conspiracies, so the notion of political assassinations still clouded her mind even in this cold, hard climate.

Deng started laughing softly and tapped her round nose gently with his finger. He casually recited a poem by Lord Byron to her:

> There is a mystic thread of life
> So dearly wreath'd with mine alone,
> That Destiny's relentless knife
> At once must sever both, or none.

A day later Zhang Jingjiang, accompanied by Sun Ke, came to visit Sun Yat-sen. When Dr. Sun saw the ailing and fragile revolutionary who had rushed from Shanghai to Beijing, he pushed himself up and feebly scolded, "Why have you made the trip when you yourself are so ill?"

The effort of uttering these words turned his face ashen white. His pulse went from 128 all the way up to 140, and his temperature soared to 39 degrees. The red light in front of his bed started to blink; the resident doctor requested that the visitors leave, and he immediately gave Dr. Sun a injection of tranquilizer.

His clenched fists gradually unfurled. The sound of phlegm could be heard in the recess of his throat but his breathing became steadier. The doctor discovered that the corners of Dr. Sun's eyes were moist with tears.

That evening Sun Yat-sen finally agreed to his wife's plea to start taking Chinese herbal medicine, but he insisted that he be released from the hospital first. He was still aware enough to recognize that using Chinese remedies in a Western hospital was not only contrary to his beliefs but an affront to the profession he had chosen all those years ago.

One of the good things about the end of the Cultural Revolution was that she could put on her spectacles and read essays commemorating Deng again.

She was elated to see the publication of *The Collected Writings of Deng Yanda*. A girlish smile appeared on her wrinkled face as she sat upright in her chair and wrote in careful calligraphy, "The publication of this work is in honor of comrade Deng Yanda for his diligence and bravery."

In the downstairs of her home in Beijing was a new projection room. She watched the old classic *Blue Angel* over and over again. The female lead, Marlene Dietrich, reminded her of Berlin after the First World War. The city was dilapidated and in ruins but a decadent air of hedonism prevailed. It was there, from 1929 to 1931, that she fell in love with thin potato cakes, the sound of melancholic German folk songs, and consorted with the man who embodied the heroic image in her heart.

Deng had embarked on a journey to the ends of the world, stopping only occasionally in Berlin. His tracks covered Poland, Lithuania, and Bulgaria as well as Turkey and India. During those two years Deng had gone as far as the North Pole, making him the first Asian ever to venture to the northernmost place on the map.

Winter came. She lit a little stove inside the projection room. Through the thin walls she could still hear the sound of the wind howling. She watched another old classic over and over; this time it was *Wuthering Heights*. The bleak black-and-white scenes did not recall her deceased husband but rather . . . God knows, she had been worried sick about the safety of Deng.

Between dried cracked lips she recited the words in the film:

Come follow me, just don't leave me in this deep pit where I can't find you.

Her beating heart longed to break through the confines of the room and fly away with the northern wind.

She did not believe in everlasting life. The rims of her eyes reddened as she gazed at the screen. The only thing that could transcend death was love.

Waking up in the middle of a long night, she remembered how desperate and crazy she had been when she left Shanghai for Nanjing. She couldn't stop shivering; her entire being called out for Deng.

It was one of the few instances when she had pushed herself almost to a point of no return. All she wanted to do was save him. She did not care at all about her position or her reputation. She chose the road of no return.

But she eventually returned to Shanghai. She did not cry; she was numb and silent. Many years later she would still remember what utter despair had felt like.

She heard later how Deng had died. He was led out of the secret chamber and strangled to death by cables. Apparently it is possible during strangulation for the prisoner to struggle bit by bit while the air is forced out bit by bit.

She rushed to Nanjing, but later she realized the tragedy had already taken place. She had made her plea for a dead man and had stomached people's jabs at her for nothing. They told her they were forced to execute a rebel in order to protect her good reputation.

Back in Shanghai the telegram that she sent to the newspaper *Shen Bao* expressed great emotion: "The staunchest revolutionary belief has been butchered and declared dead—the best example being the murder of Deng Yanda. Here lies a true, brave, and loyal revolutionary.

"I simply cannot bear to see Dr. Sun's forty years of work being devoured by a pack of selfish, manipulative Nationalist militants."

She wasn't sure how she managed to survive after Deng's death. Sometimes when she woke up, she was surprised to discover she was still breathing. In the days that followed, she tried to exorcise her memory of him. She tried to keep as busy as possible to see if the pain could somehow subside. She built a hospital, formed the People's Rights Protection Alliance, and participated in all sorts of volunteer work. She even assisted in delivering ammunition and medical supplies to the red zones. She couldn't stand to see herself so lost and helpless.

In 1933, when she finally felt she was making headway in her human rights work and that Deng would be proud of her achievements, the main supporter of the People's Rights Protection Alliance, Yang Xingfo, was assassinated.

Although she felt the same despair wash over her, there was one difference. The two of them were only comrades-in-arms, not lovers. When Deng was murdered, her only thought had been to die too.

She began to realize more and more how truly fragile the thread of life is. Dr. Sun's eyes were shut as his stretcher was carried down the hospital corridor. His face resembled that of a prophet who was enduring the final stages of persecution. The comrades in the waiting room whispered among themselves: "Dr. Sun is so pale that he already looks dead."

After the car left the hospital, it drove straight to his headquarters. With an ice pack on his forehead, Sun was at times lucid and at times confused. He thought he saw houses made out of wood outside the car window and that reminded him of the Japanese Umeyashiki Hotel, which was next to the Taipei train station. After docking at Tamsui, one could take the train to this popular hotel. He liked the Umeyashiki for its elegance and simplicity. What a shame that Taiwan had been ceded to Japan; the Japanese were suspicious and fearful about anything associated with the word *revolution*. Quite a few times officials in Taiwan had denied him the chance to move around freely.

In the next instant Sun's thoughts took him to London. He could see the Qing Legation with the heavily barred doors and windows. This was where he had been taken hostage in the early days. He felt a little embarrassed about the English account called *Kidnapped in London* that he had later written. He had exaggerated the manner in which he had been dragged into the legation office straight from the streets. He had made the whole ordeal far more dramatic than it was, and if future generations were to read his story, they would probably see how the story didn't make sense at times. Was it carelessness that had caused him to walk inside the grounds without paying heed to the dangers therein? Or had he been tricked and cajoled into going? In the old days he had used his tendency to "adapt" the story to get his message across. Naturally, there are many sides to a story. His teacher and savior had described him as someone who constantly felt he would die a cruel death. Perhaps this sense of diminishing time, as well as the desire to further the revolutionary cause, had prompted him to occasionally resort to manipulation. Of course, now it happened only on rare occasions. His alliance with Russia was an example of forced choice. In matters of alliance Dr. Sun had always been flexible. He naturally wanted to join forces with other nations; actually, not long before, he had been debating whether he should go to the Japanese or the British first. Two years earlier, during the spring, he had made the mistaken judgment of turning to Britain for foreign aid. His son and his cohorts in the party, including the likes of Wu Zhaozhu and Fu Bingchang, were to act as go-betweens and attempt to obtain some funding from a Hong Kong businessman. Who would have thought that the lender would be so greedy that **he** would ask for full control of Guangdong's finances in return? No country, it would seem, was interested in helping Sun Yat-sen solely out of the goodness of its heart. Except for Russia, no country thus far had even been willing to bet on him. Now Russia was his only way out.

When he cocked his head to listen, he thought he could clearly hear, in the wind howling outside, the voices of his opponents. They were against his alliance with Russia. They spurned his move to paint China red and they spat on his move toward the left. No, Sun protested wordlessly, what he was after was simply aid from Russia. As for his goals—he wanted this land to become wholly autonomous. He had never swayed from this belief. He had always known what he would have to sacrifice in order to achieve it. He recalled the brilliant orator Borodin, the red activist who had been sent over by the Comintern to assist Dr. Sun. They weren't even real friends. His eyes would water from the cloud of cigarette smoke that always followed Borodin. He had a habit of peppering Dr. Sun with questions or exhortations:

"So, Dr. Sun, what's your final decision?"

"Dr. Sun, be careful of befriending the enemy!"

Comrades like Zhang Ji, Xie Ci, and Deng Ziru warned Dr. Sun repeatedly. He penned words of rebuke in the letters they sent him. Deng Ziru, the most vocal opponent of his association with Russia, wrote that these were critical times; Sun Yat-sen replied that indeed these were critical times, but when had it not been a critical time for their party? In the end, had it been worth it? His ties with Russia had angered more than half his comrades, including the most senior founding members. The comrades warned him that a split in the Nationalist Party would be inevitable. The warlords used Russia as a means of discrediting him. The masses in the North never forgave him. In his final days he seemed to hear all the voices opposing him. Nonetheless, Sun refused to believe that the voices of dissent he was hearing now would be louder than the laments of sorrow that would follow a month later. At his funeral many civic organizations hung calligraphy scrolls from the beams to memorialize him. Young schoolgirls broke down in tears when his coffin passed. Students from Beijing University sent wreaths to honor him, while students from the Sino-French University erected a white banner inscribed with the words *Sun Yat-sen Lives On*. To the masses the death of the tragic patriot before the blueprint of the Republic had been realized was a wake-up call. When his body passed the buildings on Xidan, people climbed up telephone poles just to get one last look at him. The four white flags at the left end of the road represented the National Railway Association.

The railroad men never forgot Dr. Sun and Dr. Sun never forgot the railways. Although the days he spent sprawled over maps, marking different locations, were a thing of the past, he still thought back to those golden years. He had just stepped down from his position as president and was consumed by his railway plans. Sun had always been a dreamer. With a pencil and a small eraser in his hand, he would draw up the three main rail lines on the map of China: the Southern Line, the Central Line, and the Northern Line. The Southern Line would cut through small mountain paths to the remote villages of Tibet before reaching Tianshan in Xinjiang. Sun Yat-sen would seize every opportunity to talk about his dream of laying 200,000 miles of railroad tracks in ten years so that China could be free from poverty forever. He used the United States as an example. Whenever Sun Yat-sen mentioned the railways, his spirits would soar. Excitedly, he would inform the journalist interviewing him that before the railways were built, the United States had been as poor as China. However, after the

Americans built the three-thousand-mile intercontinental railroad, theirs became the wealthiest country in the world!

He struggled to open his eyes inside the slow-moving car. The view outside seemed bleak and gray. He couldn't see a hint of green in the winter palette of the North. In the next instant he remembered his experience in Japan. At dusk the train rode slowly through the valley. The train window reflected like a mirror as daylight faded. His face floated between the reflections of clumps of trees. When they came out of the valley, a ray of sunlight struck the floor of the compartment. His still-youthful face had blurred against the window. He longed for a time when China would be joined together by railway and boast clean and comfortable compartments like the ones he had been in.

He wanted to wallow in the sensory delights of old memories and forget how his body ached all over. He recalled the reflection of the Golden Shrine in Kyoto against the water in a corner of the garden. At the end of his life journey, how could he tell the comrades next to him that the city he wanted to see one last time was Kyoto? He also yearned to see the cremation grounds near Asakusa in Tokyo, where mounds of deities and stones were piled high. He had often strolled there in the winter to savor the melancholic rites of the Japanese. Although he often made utterances such as " the politicians in Japan tend to look down on our party" and "the Japanese politicians are too short-sighted and they do not practice what they preach; we would do well to go with the Russians instead," many things about Japan still were familiar and benign to him. Who had written the haiku from the Edo period?

> Old age
> To relinquish desire
> What sorrow.

His thoughts turned to Ohtsuki Kaoru from Yokohama, with her budding breasts and fifteen-year-old body. She liked to wear clothes that had a sailor collar, and her voice had a slight lilt to it. She possessed an irresistible charm—her cheeks were constantly flushed and her skin was poreless. The first time he held her in his arms, she curled up like a cat. Even though she didn't resist him, he still had to do quite a bit of coaxing before she stretched out on the tatami mat. The slight tremor of her naked breasts resembled the pale snow on Fuji Mountain. He was amazed at her youth, and, holding her, he could smell the soft sweet scent of a young girl who was offering up herself to him. Sun Yat-sen used his lips to explore every inch of her untouched skin. He had never felt such temptation. He had been a completely ignorant boy of twenty on his wedding night. Her armpits started to perspire and she called out " Takano-san!"—Dr. Sun's Japanese name. He felt a little trepidation; she didn't even know his real name, yet she still idolized this man lying on top of her. She was fully consumed by hero worship. When he thought of her adoring looks, Sun felt the life flow back into him. After all, hadn't his years of experience proved to him that failure was only a prelude to a new beginning? Despite his present exhaustion, Dr. Sun believed he still had a chance and he could still win.

She exuded a kind of feminine detachment that drew men to her. In the eyes of purists who were new to the game and who were willing to sacrifice everything for the revolution, Madame Sun's marblelike countenance held undeniable appeal. In their eyes she was the untarnished flower that grew out of mud and possessed only one tragic flaw: the men to whom she had given her heart had all died.

Her appeal also had a certain urgency to it. She was a woman of forty, a flower in full bloom at the cusp of wilting.

As the clock ticked away, these idealistic suitors understood that the greatest danger lay not in defeat at the hands of the enemy but that, in the very next minute, your faith could be turned on its head when you least expected it.

She knew all along that fate wanted her alive. During times of danger her disguise had been an expression of a bewildered naïvété. It was her protective coloring. During a life of incessant upheaval, her innocent-looking face seemed untouched by reality.

She often recalled the American-looking ice cream parlor in the middle of Shanghai's Nanjing Road. At the height of the Alliance's work, she was in the habit of meeting friends there because fewer people were keeping tabs on her there. Many years later she could still visualize through closed eyes the moment that Edgar Snow had pushed open the glass door. His tie was hung loosely around his neck, and his freckled face with chestnut-colored eyes was all smiles. Back then Snow had not yet begun working in the red zone nor had he written *Red Star over China*. He was working simply on celebrity profiles.

A few days after they had met, she read in the newspaper the words that this young American journalist, twelve years her junior, had used to describe his enchantment with her. He wrote, "In person, Madame Sun looks 10 years younger than her actual age." In the next paragraph Snow says the biggest surprise to him as a journalist was to discover "the huge ambivalence that existed between her appearance and her fate."

Sitting in her rocking chair, she opened her eyes. She was truly getting on in years. . . . She had thought of a face from her past only because Snow's ex-wife Helen had come to China again. Many rules had been relaxed after the Cultural Revolution, but the funny thing was that she had no desire to meet with Helen.

Her fingers touched the lines etched on her face. Time waits for no one, she sighed wordlessly.

Edgar Snow had already passed away. She refused Helen Snow's request to visit her, which had been written on a sheet of paper that had been shoved under her door. Would her decision have been different if it were Edgar Snow who had come to China? Would she have met with him? Her pen stopped in midsentence.

She stood up carefully and moved about with great difficulty. She took a book down from the shelf. Under the dim light she caressed the yellowing pages. On the overleaf of the book Snow had written the words:

To S.Q.L.
  For her perseverance, courage and beauty of spirit;
  She is the brightest and most exemplary symbol of China.

43

Lying in the inner sanctum of the house, Ma Xiang read the Chinese doctor Lu Zhongan's prescription to Dr. Sun. He listened with distaste but felt too weak to say anything. He groaned softly, desperately needing morphine. Only morphine could lull him to sleep.

As the pain medication took effect, Dr. Sun thought that he had always been too polite to Hu Shi, to the point that Hu had had the audacity to recommend a Chinese doctor to him. Sun Yat-sen was a true believer in Western science, even though many scholars well versed in matters of the West often betrayed him when he most needed their support. Hu had used his pen to criticize Sun more than once in the newspapers of the North. During the period when Sun was at loggerheads with Chen Jiongming, Hu had written an article entitled "The Corpse of Old Morality" in which he blamed Dr. Sun for forming a political party based on archaic dogma. In Hu's mind Sun Yat-sen was wrong in banishing Chen just because he had dared to betray his superior. Sun was forced to counter this thesis on various occasions by saying, "Today those who advocate 'new culture' completely look down on traditional culture. They think that they can relinquish the old just because there is something new." He was determined not to pander to these high-minded, theoretical scholars. Sun had made up his mind that he was going to ignore Hu and not pay any attention to the supposedly renowned Beijing doctor before him. "Hu Shi, you know I studied Western medicine," was all Dr. Sun said behind closed eyes. With that he turned Hu's offer down.

Standing awkwardly on the side, his wife suddenly interjected, "Seeing as the doctor's already here, why don't you let him briefly examine you?" There was no way he could say no to her almost begging tone of voice. He sighed and with some effort turned his face toward the whitewashed wall. The doctor sat next to his bed and placed his cool fingers on his wrist. He then wrote down the prescription with the various Chinese herbal ingredients on it. On the same piece of paper he had also written "fear and anger have seriously damaged his liver." Could one really interpret the body based on the murmur of a pulse? Deep down, he knew what fatal emotions lodged in his heart. In the last few years people's mockery and cold-shouldered treatment had indeed wounded him. In the end, he had sacrificed his youth but gained little sympathy. People blamed him for swinging from left to right; they scoffed that he was all appearance and no substance. They intoned that if China needed totalitarianism to become strong, then Dr. Sun would become a totalitarian. If China needed socialism, Dr. Sun would probably take shortcuts to become a ruler who embraced Leninist beliefs as well.

But who understood what he had given up to bring the people together? He did all he could to prevent the separation of leftist and rightist comrades. Perhaps he had been too hasty in lumping socialism with people's welfare, but he had quickly taken to heart the success of the revolution in Russia. At the same time he knew that he had to reduce the suspicion of the traditionalists. To do that, he linked the three principles of the people with traditional philosophies. Of the people, for the people—and he pulled in Confucius and Mencius for good measure. In a letter he had written to a friend, he had said, "The idea of a Soviet is the same as the principle of universality that Confucius endorsed. Why do we need to fear something as simple and clear as that?" In truth, Dr. Sun's aim was to merge the East with the West. His early training as a doctor made him dislike anything that was too abstract. He was inclined toward a melding of practical philosophies. In matters of uncertainty his position had always been to walk the middle road. Many years before he had used a wise analogy: "The North is like the old lunar calendar while the South is like the new solar calendar. We need to use both calendars together. One without the other wouldn't work."

In this vast land, using different calendars was like listening to the sounds of different clocks ticking. In order to accommodate the present situation Sun Yat-sen had to constantly bow his head in compromise. He had paid a very high price, but what did he have to show for it? He had been wronged to the point that people said he was willing to compromise with the Japanese at one point. They said that under the banner of "Pan Asia," Dr. Sun had given the Japanese rights to China on the condition that they join forces in fighting the Western nations. Even Huang Xing had asked Feng Ciyou to advise Sun not to sacrifice the larger picture for small gains. Sun gave a heavy sigh—let them say what they want. Compared with Huang Xing, he had always been considered wayward. The comrades from the old school had always seen Huang Xing, with his writing talents, as being much more approachable than Sun. They had faith in Huang Xing's gentlemanly demeanor. At his funeral many eulogies hinted that here was a man who with great humility had relinquished the leadership position to Sun. Members of the intelligentsia felt much closer to Huang Xing in every way.

The more Sun thought about it, the more defeated he felt. He had failed to find allies. Not only did Westernized scholars such as Hu Shi not respect him, foreigners were the same. They constantly used the stringent standards of democracy to criticize Dr. Sun for being too domineering. When comrades were told to call him "Sir," they felt that Dr. Sun was advocating a form of "sacred leadership." They thought he saw his fellow comrades as disciples or Confucian students who were forbidden to see any wrong in their teacher. Actually, his instincts were accurate. Many foreign scholars studying Sun Yat-sen's life at a later date refused to give him a fair assessment. The kinder critics, like Clarence Martin Wilbur, called him a "frustrated patriot," which later actually became the subtitle of his book. The less kind, such as Harold Z. Schiffrin, commented bluntly, "If he possessed any talent, it was the ability to fail time and again." People like Lyon Sharman said Sun was a leader who lacked judgment and consistently placed the wrong person in the wrong place. As for the Russian military expert Borodin, he had it in his mind that Dr. Sun was someone who saw himself as a hero and people around him as part of the ignorant masses. In actual fact, that was the common view of the Comintern—even Lenin mocked Dr. Sun for being naive and ignorant, like a lady-in-waiting. But let's not forget that these were scholars who were looking at a weak and flailing nation from the vantage point of Russia. They didn't really care about China. They never spoke of China without derision. Did they care how poverty-stricken and ill her people were? Not for a single second. But he did. The hardship suffered by the people was his greatest cause of defeat. He had personally witnessed soldiers so poor that they had to walk barefoot. He had experienced the bullying of imperialism first hand.

It was a blisteringly cold northern winter outside, and the morphine triggered memories of warlords who had aligned themselves with imperialism. They used every possible means to attack him and defame his achievements. Sun Yat-sen had never been a quitter; he persisted in continuing the Northern Expedition because his blueprint for building China had never been restricted to one province or one region. He had always wanted to save this vulnerable piece of land in its entirety. But now he was about to bow out of the power game. When fresh snow fell again on the northern territory, his lifetime endeavors would be completely buried. Had he been wrong? He had been left out of the game simply because he didn't have command of the forces or a belief in totalitarianism? The self-efficient and strong map of China that he had envisaged building had shrunk once again to its prerevolution size.

He saw the shadow of visitors outside his door. He cleared his throat and asked who had come. Ma Xiang told him that committees had already been set up to see to the arrival of visitors. Even at the very end Sun never found out who, other than his closest friends, had come to visit him out of courtesy and who had come out of true reverence for him. Initially, he had hoped the leaders in the North would drop by to see him, but he no longer had the energy to care.

In the next instant he thought he heard voices outside his door. He opened his eyes and saw the morning light peering past the curtains. His eyes touched on a wall clock ticking away; he pondered what he could still do. He longed to order time to stand still. Ever since his old friend Wu Ting-fang had died, Sun had stopped sitting in front of the chessboard, but he still remembered the possibility in chess to reverse a losing game. If only he had a little more time to think things through. . . .

Sadly, the clock inside him was no longer willing to wait. It was ticking away faster and faster, moving steadily to the day that would later become National Arbor Day.

She had grown even older—sometimes she found it hard to believe she had lived this long.

Some of the books she had moved over from Shanghai belonged to her husband. The layer of dust that coated their covers made them seem so remote to her.

She tried to remember what things excited her. A joke? The appealing face of a young man? A box of chocolates from abroad or a stimulating debate? Many years ago she had liked to hear witty repartee. She had always preferred eloquent people.

Her dentures did not fit well. She could eat only the softest, most tasteless food. Back in the old days she had been adept at swimming, horseback riding, and driving. She found it hard to believe what her youth had been like.

Staring at the image of Sun in the photographs, she envied him for not having to survive old age and suffer the consequences.

What depressed her was the need to still play games with those who wanted to exploit her. She really disliked the presence of these people. They dutifully called her "Chief" to her face but behind her back? She had no doubt these new citizens of China had another side to them that she could not see. Nobody could fool her! In front of others her voice sounded flat and harsh; she was accustomed to giving them the cold shoulder.

There was no way they were going to find her weaknesses. She never signed her letters or addressed them. She always immediately destroyed her notes. In the past when she had to save leftist intellectuals, she had learned quite a bit about the ins and outs of underground work.

She used the tinkle of a bell to summon people who worked for her.

One of their important tasks was to watch the classics with her. Inside the projection room on the first floor she would watch the films over and over again, experiencing the same emotions with each viewing.

Three mornings a week she would summon a masseuse from the Beijing Hotel. Sometimes her body still felt stiff after the massage. She thought yearningly of S's hands, which moved with great agility over her body.

She squeezed her eyes tightly and tried to remember the best things about Shanghai: spiced beans and white rabbit toffee. She would hand these goodies out to the servants who dutifully woke up just before the end of each film.

The only two people in the world who could get her to laugh out loud were the sisters Yuyu and Zenzen. She had gone to great lengths to arrange for them to stay with her at the residence. The older sister, Yuyu, always had a trick up her sleeve and did her best to make Madame Sun happy. When she had to pose for a photograph or meet visitors, Yuyu would hide Madame's false teeth away and pretend they were lost. At the very last minute she would suddenly stuff the dentures quickly into the old lady's mouth. Madame Sun would burst out laughing and play childish peek-a-boo games with Yuyu and Zenzen.

When Yuyu would frequent Friendship Stores with her boyfriend or use a credit card at a coffee shop, outsiders would rush to tell Madame Sun about it. "Don't fret about it!" she would call out and silence the person before he had the chance to finish his sentence. She wanted the sisters to know that she was not so senile that she could be manipulated.

No one really understood how she felt. How could those spies know what those two girls gave her? Whether they amounted to much was one thing, but at least they would kneel before her lap and caress her craggy face with their soft youthful palms.

"They're misleading you, but we know better!" people would say before launching into an account about how extravagant and spoiled Yuyu was behaving. Consternation washed over Madame Sun. She had weathered countless scams in her life. In this instance she would willingly be misled.

A distant overseas relative told her about her younger sister, who was living on Long Island. The relative intoned, "She is very lonely, and her beauty is fading too . . . sometimes even bathing in milk has its limits." The relative went on to say with mock horror that, according to the old servants in the house, when her sister let her hair down to sleep at night, she resembled a frightful ghost.

The relative probably thought he was making Madame Sun happy, but she actually felt a strange sense of sorrow. This was her poor sister, who was four years younger than she. . . . She remembered her own countenance when she let her hair down to sleep at night. Only a woman as old as she was could truly empathize with another woman almost the same age.

What lay beyond her walls? The Shi Cha Lake or Yinding Bridge? The old allies of Beijing? The tall walls hid a whole world from her vision.

She had been bedridden for the last little while. Her legs were so bloated they couldn't touch the ground. She felt like a concubine who had been left to rot in the recesses of the palace. She, the aging concubine of a deceased emperor, was living in an abandoned aristocrat's residence.

The rain continued to fall outside her window. The irony of her fate made her laugh out loud; she laughed until her eyes were two mere slits. Her choked laughter reverberated against the warm tears on her cheeks. Suddenly, she was transported beyond the gates and saw the rainbow hues of glass reflected in the puddles of rainwater.

On February 28, 1925, the paper *China News* in Hong Kong reported, "Dr. Sun's situation is stable. He slept well last night and is in good spirits. He experienced slight diarrhea after taking his Chinese medication."

In the *Father of the Nation Chronicles,* compiled by the Nationalist Party History Center, Sun Yat-sen is said to have mentioned Chiang Kai-shek's name numerous times during this period. Sun received news of Chiang's victories frequently, and Wang Jingwei, who was looking after Dr. Sun at the time, even wrote a telegram to the president of the Whampoa Military Academy that read, "Dear Kai-shek, after receiving your telegram from Tamsui, I read it sentence by sentence to our premier. He drew great comfort from your message and has asked me to write back on his behalf. He wants to commend all officers involved for a job well done. Keep it up. Our earnest hope is for the 'Three Principles of the People' to be realized in time. With best wishes, Wang Jingwei."

Every so often visitors would call. This time the State Department said her old friend Ellison wanted to see her.

How long had it been?

Shanghai. French Quarters. Number 29, Moliere Street. Mrs. Smetterley had introduced an American Jewish sympathizer to her. The first time they met, she could feel his blue eyes boring into her as they watched her every move. He was barely twenty; she had been a widow of forty.

Even now she pretended not to know of his infatuation with her. Of course, she knew this silvery-haired professor before her with moist eyes was trying to recall what she had been like, in the same way she knew when they first met that he harbored romantic feelings for her.

The smile emanating from her tired eyes was still the same—benign but aloof, exercising extreme self-control. Deep down she was touched. On his first visit she remembered cautioning the naive young man in her spacious home, "You have to be careful of the people in Beijing."

"Are you referring to the Nationalist Party?"

"Not just the party. Beware even those you think are friends." It was unusual for her to speak from the heart. She went on, "The political circles are extremely complicated. Anything could happen."

The second time around, her servants had propped her up to meet her visitor in the living room. She wanted to talk only about the girls. She interrupted Ellison in the middle of his reminiscences and remarked smilingly, "Let me tell you about my newfound relatives, Yuyu and Zenzen."

Later she received an English book sent from abroad. It was *My China Years*, written by Helen Snow after she had returned home to the United States. Madame Sun leafed through the pages and read about Helen's disappointment at not seeing her on her last trip. She also chronicled the state of Song's former home in the French section of Shanghai and the details of their last meeting forty years earlier, including the wedding present, a silver coffeepot, that Madame Sun had given Helen and Edgar. In the section that described Madame Sun, Helen marveled, "In a life where she could have had anything she wanted, Madame Sun chose the road of solitude and danger. Why is that?"

She caressed the cover of the book and wondered whether she could indeed have had anything she wanted.

In retrospect the road she had traveled had been the one that many avoided. The irony was that no one had ever told her there was an easier alternative.

National policies grew more and more lax.

With the approval of the government she commissioned Epstein, the foreigner who had applied for Chinese citizenship, to pen her memoirs. After the Cultural Revolution he had become the editor-in-chief of the revamped propaganda magazine *China Construction*. She smiled to herself. She was sure her old friend knew how to glorify the deceased; she had faith in him.

Several foreign publishers had tried to get in touch with her. A U.S. publishing house had agreed to give her $500,000 if she would write an autobiography. She told Yuyu and Zenzen jokingly, "Let's give it some thought—we're talking about $500,000 here!"

She knew she wouldn't be leaving anything in writing. She was a completely disillusioned old woman. She did not have any designs on the world in which she now lived.

Even now Sun Yat-sen refused to believe that death was imminent. His neck was limp and lifeless, and the heels of his feet were swollen. When he lay on his side, his arms would automatically fall forward. Looking at him, Ma Xiang realized that even the most casual gestures required some degree of exertion. However, Sun was still able to speak. When Ma Xiang put his ear next to the leader's mouth, he heard him call out, "Shi Gu, Shi Gu." Dr. Sun used to be acutely aware of the smell of perspiration on her body. Was she still cooking and washing clothes for former comrades? Droplets of sweat slid off the ends of her hair and fell to her cheek; hers was a musky sweet smell. His memory of her had nothing to do with gratitude; rather it was one of a profound regret because he had given her nothing. At least his first wife, Lu, had been left with a son and a daughter, even after their older daughter had died. His children had always been closer to their mother than to him. As for his young wife, Qingling, she may be losing the protection of her husband but at least she had received a complete education in her youth, and she still had a large family to go back to. That left Shi Gu, a woman who asked for nothing from him.

"Shi Gu," Dr. Sun's whisper was as soft as a sigh. Ma Xiang put his hand over Dr. Sun's burning hand and was surprised by its dry heat. Dr. Sun murmured her name, "Shi Gu, Xiangling, Chen Cuifen." They had known each other a long time—back in the days of the South Pacific and Yokohama, Japan, when he was constantly on the road. That the most depressing period of his revolutionary career. Sun remembered that she had rough hands, round buttocks, and the skin on her nipple had been dark brown and wrinkled. Whenever he got ready to leave, she would never ask him where he was going, except once. The evening before the battle at Chengnan Gate, they had downed a few cups of wine as a gesture of farewell. The rims of Shi Gu's eyes had reddened, and she had refused to loosen her grip on Dr. Sun's shoulders. *Which year had that been?* He couldn't remember. *Did they meet again at a later date?* He couldn't recall that, either. All he knew was that she had never married. What had he given her? Dr. Sun remembered that he once gave her a gold watch given to him by Mr. Cantlie. Apparently, Shi Gu often showed it to people who went to see her. He repeated her name as he lay in bed; he did not want to forget the woman who had been part of his virile, insouciant youth.

Standing in front of the bed, Ma Xiang noticed Dr. Sun's bare arms. Green veins protruded from his pale skin. Many years later Ma would write in his memoirs that he could still remember the color of Dr. Sun's excrement and how hollow his body felt after embalming. But at this moment Ma was convinced that Dr. Sun would get better because two months earlier Sun Yat-sen was still in perfect health. Ma had followed Dr. Sun to many places, and they had shared many precious memories. Ma had originally been an overseas swordsman from Hong Men. He had undergone life-threatening situations with Dr. Sun more than once. He liked to recount a time in Wuzhou when Sun had climbed Wan Fu Mountain to go to the lookout and one of his ski poles had snapped. Dr. Sun slid down the hill with Ma's arm cushioning his fall. Ma suffered a few scrapes on his arms but Dr. Sun was unscathed. This story grew more perilous with every telling. Ma was proud that he had had a chance to protect and look after Dr. Sun during those few years. Suddenly, as if by miracle, he heard Sun's voice: "Help me sit up."

Ma put his hands under Dr. Sun's legs to prop him up. He was so much lighter than before. Ma placed Sun on the window ledge and bent down to gently massage his left foot. The swelling still hadn't gone down. His stomach was bloated and his muscles had lost their resilience. His flesh already felt waxy.

That afternoon Dr. Sun's temperature did not suddenly soar as it had on previous days. After seeing his complexion, many believed the Chinese medicine was taking effect and a miracle had actually taken place. What's more, Dr. Sun even asked for some grapes to eat. Ma Xiang drove his car all over Beijing and returned near nightfall with the few bunches of grapes he had found.

When the grape skin was removed, someone put a grape into Dr. Sun's mouth. The muscles near his mouth twitched and he started to cough badly. He hadn't even managed to swallow the grape before he vomited black bile from his stomach.

Sometimes light beams crossed and then separated in her dreams, causing her swollen face to flush an unnatural red. Against the rapid patter of rain beating down on the windowpane, she would mutter incoherently in her sleep. With a jerk she would wipe away the traces of saliva around the corners of her mouth when a flash of lightning suddenly grazed the midnight sky.

During these half-asleep and half-awake hours, her eyes would land on a photograph of Sun Yat-sen on the wall. When lightning struck a second time, she discovered that her own face was starting to look more and more like her husband's. Their even features, their round chin seemed almost sexless in appearance . . . her eyes roamed from the head down to the drooping mouth before giving up . . . old age had robbed her of all her physical advantages. The path of old age ended in sameness.

She needed to find ways to pass the time. During her bed-bound hours she started to think of the exact moment when she had started to age. Even though her legs were numb, her mind was still lucid. She reflected on the roles she had played throughout her life. In the early years people liked to see her as the nubile young wife in stories surrounding Dr. Sun. Worse yet, they sometimes viewed her as just a burial piece lying in a pretty satin box or a stuffed butterfly that had been pinned to the wall. God knows how hard she had tried to dispel these impressions! She had wanted to prove she was more than just Dr. Sun's widow.

The funny thing was, during the last few years the situation seemed to have reversed. Although the Cultural Revolution was now a thing of the past, her husband's status had yet to be restored. Regardless of whether she liked the role of widow or not, she was destined to serve as Dr. Sun's guardian angel. Year after year four burly men would carry her down the stairs to the big hall where she would have to read her speech at the perfunctory service commemorating his life.

In her speech she attempted to read the mind of the deceased. Her husband had never understood that the world was ultimately a wasteland. When he had passed away, she remembered his expression, as if he were not quite yet ready to part. He was hinging on the possibility the tables could still turn, that he might win and the end was not yet over.

Compared with her husband, she at least had the chance to stand on the side of the victor. She had helped establish the new socialist China. On October 1 that year, she had been one of the first to hail in the new country at the gates of Tiananmen. But as she lay in her bed, she reflected that at the end of it all no one could claim that having survived the Cultural Revolution was an ultimate victory.

She touched her liver-spotted face and thought: If victory was an illusion, what was truth? Was it her unswerving faith in the men that she loved? She was different from her husband, she reflected. She had never been concerned with how history would remember her.

"I feel . . . I have said everything I need to. If I get better, I will retreat to the hot springs; perhaps after some contemplation, I will let you know what I plan to do next. However, if my health fails . . . then do as you see fit. I have nothing . . . more to say."

With visible effort Sun uttered these words. He looked around him and thought of the one lesson he had learned all these years. What you say often comes back to haunt you. The comrades standing by his bedside had given up their differences to gather around him when they heard he had fallen ill. They had even drawn up his will and urged him to give his final words.

He looked at the slim white fingers holding out the will to him. These were not the hands of a traitor. For one second, as he cast his eyes downward, the comrades who had looked sincere and respectful just a minute before now quickly exchanged looks of warning. Dr. Sun did not care to know what could be brewing among them, just as he was too tired to ponder the kind of fight for power that would ensue when he was no longer around to serve as mediator. For the last two years the fighting inside the party had exhausted him, and to his regret very little time and effort had been given to how they could turn an impoverished land into a nation that enjoyed a balanced distribution of wealth. Sun remembered the simple yet effective single taxation system that he had devised: the more valuable the land, the heavier the tax levied. He had been an ardent supporter of Henry George's ever since he had first come into contact with George's theories twenty years before. Sun Yat-sen liked to reiterate that land monopolization was the root of all evil and the growing gap between the rich and the poor was in fact a problem of distribution. The comrades, however, lacked the interest to further this discussion. They were far more enthusiastic about factional politics. He sighed in frustration and wished he could stop thinking. In his current state he had no way of anticipating how fragmented the Nationalist Party would become down the road. In recent years he had always believed that his authority would steady the boat and that the party had to adopt a unified front in the face of the Northern Expedition. But that was now; he had no way of knowing the future. Dr. Sun recalled that in the earlier years Song Jiaoren and Huang Xing had advocated a parliamentary system, which was dismissed in favor of the presidential system that Sun had supported. Dr. Sun was worried that the dispute could recur and cause another controversy in the future. He hoped it would be only a gentlemen's debate and not result in serious rivalry between the boys.

"Enemies will surround you and try to soften you. If I say too much now, it may endanger your solidarity at a later date. I would rather remain silent and trust that you will adapt and adjust to the changing environment," Sun murmured slowly.

What was his legacy? Was it a philosophy, an ideology, or was it the spirit of the revolution? Suddenly, he heard the sound of intermittent weeping coming from his wife in the next room. What else was he leaving behind? He remembered the other will that he had been asked to sign, the domestic will. "As I have devoted most of my time to national affairs, I have not had time to manage my own assets. I hereby bequeath my remaining books, clothing, and home to my wife, Song Qingling, in memory of my life." The words were too true. He had not managed his assets and had always been careless about his belongings. In his younger days he made only enough money to buy his next train or ship ticket. Even now his only apartment in Shanghai was a donation from an overseas Chinese. Ironically, he had spent most of his life trying to raise money. He worried about the lack of funding almost on a daily basis. Mingled with his physical pain, he could still feel that same pressure hovering above him. He remembered a night in Denver when he had received a telegram requesting the urgent transfer of funds a few days before the Wuchang Uprising. Because he had left the Morse code in his bags, he deciphered the telegram only on the evening of October 10. That night he tossed and turned, not knowing how he could respond to the plea. When he read at the breakfast table the following morning news that the revolutionaries had already occupied Wuchang, his first thought was relief that he did not have to write a response. Dr. Sun sighed. Money had always been a thorn in his flesh. During the United League period in 1907 he had suffered public outrage because the party's ledger books were a mess. The editor-in-chief of the newspaper *Ming Bao,* Zhang Binglin, openly accused Dr. Sun of pocketing the money and advocated that he be expelled from the United League. He had been so wronged! He shut his eyes and winced at the memory. In later years the situation deteriorated further. In 1917, when he arrived to establish the military government in Guangzhou, the government had been completely in the red. He had no food to feed his soldiers, no guns to arm them, and no land. He was forced to depend on soldiers of fortune for favors. In name he may have been the leader of the country, but in truth he had had to obtain permission just to leave his head-quarters. All the employees in the government were handed a meager $20 allowance. Even after accepting these conditions, the military government still got rid of him in the end. Dr. Sun thought of the pitiful circumstances that his wife would have to endure after his death. Was he really expecting her to beg for money from others? Aside from the two-thousand-odd books and house he was leaving her, she didn't have a cent to her name.

He continued to hear the sound of his wife weeping. Sun didn't know what he could say to her. He felt a vague sense of sadness and loss. He knew the changes in the outside world would speed up and his widow would be left behind. Actually, what Dr. Sun failed to see was that his wife's predica-ment would not stem from money matters but rather from her despair when former comrades who had fought alongside her husband strayed from his path. He had no way of knowing that she would be exiled abroad, forced to severe family ties, and have to pronounce resolutely, "I have not lost heart in the revolution; what I find disheartening is witnessing how some of the leaders of the revolution have deviated from their cause."

At that moment his wife's weeping next door seemed particularly sor-rowful because of how hard she tried to suppress it.

She remembered how her husband had come to his end during those final two months in Beijing.

He had called her to his bedside to speak his last words. Before she had a chance to make sense of his words, which were blurred by phlegm, he had started to pant from the effort of speaking. She cried when she saw his lips moving noiselessly, until the only sound left in the room was the sound of her weeping. She held on to his hand and her body shivered half in fear. Death seemed like a current that passed from the tips of his fingers to hers.

The cigarette between her fingers went out. She sat in the middle of a dark void. It seemed as if the smell of death had crept in from the bottom of the door and spread all over the room.

She heard the music again. It was her favorite requiem.

I often pictured Madame Sun lying alone in the shadows. A witness to a century of change would lie passively in the dark without speaking. The tides of change had taught her that upbringing, countenance, and love are fickle; only betrayal and manipulation persevere.

Did her rigid body continue to wait in that big house? Did she wait until a flash of lightning streaked across the midnight sky before pressing on the keys of the piano to hear the notes of a familiar childhood melody? Was her lighted cigarette the only thing that glowed in the darkness . . . this was becoming too much like a scene in a novel . . . my own novel. . . . Actually, even if Madame Sun weren't the character in question, this had all the makings of a novel. The novel would bear no resemblance to the numerous Song Qingling biographies that have been written already. They are filled with archaic language, and one is left with no impression of the person at all.

How would I write it? I was not a novelist and . . . the evidence seemed to lead everywhere and nowhere.

In later life she was like an old woman who had lost her nerve and could make only the odd ceremonial appearance. People often described her as a bird in a golden cage; she had no contact with the outside world and no freedom to speak of.

I looked up; the antique birdcage collected by Simpson's mother was in front of me.

I pitied Madame Sun. Even though she detested that huge garden near the Shi Cha Hai Lake, she could not leave it. She was like a bird that had been so long in captivity that she would to lose her way if she were set free.

52

A day later Dr. Sun fell into a coma.

He barely swallowed the beef gruel and ginseng soup that had been prepared for him. He had lost his sense of taste. At the same time his mind
wandered back and forth in time. Even though his parents were a dusty,
distant memory, he still thought of Sun Mei—his older brother who often
liked to scold him. Sun Mei had given up most of his wealth and posses-
sions in support of the revolution. Dr. Sun opened his eyes. Did he just
dream about the house he had designed for himself? He felt his presence
haunt the corridors like an apparition. The warm breeze he had felt against
the backdrop of coconut trees was totally different from the icicles hanging
from the eaves of the old Chinese-style building before him. He was sure
that in the last few days, as he drifted in and out of consciousness, rumors
about his death abounded in the South. No, he was not ready to quit. He
cared about the military developments in Dongjiang, and he was still waiting to hear about his troops' victory in the North. As long as he breathed,
he would not allow the Republic to be an empty husk. It wasn't his fault . . .
Lord knows how he had tried to make the most of every opportunity. In
his dreams he saw his mouth gaping open as he tried to defend himself.
What was he trying to say? His was a case of the right person at the wrong
time. All his efforts had gotten him nowhere. He had been so persistent
about the goal of unification, yet, after five years of the Republic, he was
still struggling to gain a foothold in Guangdong Province. These thoughts
came and went; his breathing became more irregular. Sun remembered
what he had said to the American consul, Shulman: "I am not a warlord,

I am a doctor and in my eyes, wars are like fighting evil with evil." He was constantly trying to correct people's mistaken perceptions about him. Was this Guangzhou, 1923? He had been foolish and naive in mistaking the southwest warlords for compatriots. He recalled that it had been a very difficult spring for him. He moved his mouth to ask the silent question: "Am I an aristocrat or simply a poor, ignorant kid from Corsica?" Was he already exiled to an island? Sun remembered the passage that he had read in Napoleon's autobiography; every time he recalled Napoleon's words, he felt deeply moved. Suddenly, he moaned as a sharp stab of pain interrupted his contemplation. What did he end up achieving? He told himself that he must have created or gained something after surviving all these hardships and failure. What was it? He had created a country . . . or was it just a dream of a country? He had devoted himself to setting the future blueprint for this country: the transportation networks, the ports, the railways, the paved roads that spread throughout the central, northern, and southern parts of China. These regions were to have a port as big as New York. Along the coast he planned to develop commercial and fishing harbors. He was going to plant forests, make steel, irrigate Mongolia and Xinjiang, as well as have people populate the three provinces in the East.

"If my vision can be realized, then China will no longer be a dumping ground for the rest of the world but will become the main ocean of prosperity." In his mind he thought he saw blurred ink on a piece of paper. Was his wife still busy writing down his "nation-building strategies"?

In the next instant he felt her small cool hand on his forehead. He opened his eyes and gazed at this woman who had stood by his side all this time. She moved with easy grace and spoke in a gentle, soft hush. She was even more beautiful now that she had lost weight. At this moment how he longed to give his life over to his darling Rosamund. This rush of feeling was rare for him; he quickly remembered that he wasn't leaving behind just one widow but three. Madame Sun, Madame Lu. and Shi Gu or, rather, Madame Chen had all waited in vain for him all these years. There were other women whose faces he couldn't quite recall. The geisha called Shizuko, who was the major drawing card at the Umeyashiki restaurant. Dr. Sun remembered how he had sat cross-legged on the tatami mat as he sipped his wine. He had been a tired but active revolutionary at the time. Aside from keeping in touch with his comrades, he had needed to maintain a constant high. During the early years he often feasted his eyes on breasts as pale as cream in the tiny motel in Chinatown. In the heat of passion he would push himself on top of the girl. . . . But now, he closed his eyes in impotence. . . .

Suddenly, sound died down. "Master Sun has passed away!" He heard the rush of footsteps and gasps of shock. They were probably getting ready to resuscitate him. He could feel the doctor injecting something into his limp arm at the side of the bed. Strangely, he could see himself rising out of his bed and looking at everything from above . . . his arm lay across the bureau, looking like a piece of shriveled, hairless pork leg.

He heard the clock strike twelve. Another day had come and gone. "At least I still have another day," he muttered to himself. He knew his decision not to sign a will the day before had been right.

53

She had no desire to be buried in Nanjing beside her husband. After a lifetime of upheaval that was not her wish.

She thought of her husband lying in the casket for people to pay tribute to him. The long gown and mandarin jacket he had worn made him look like an ancient scholar. If death was a gradual descent, she felt her husband was sinking into profound lethargy.

Ultimately, women were different from men. Once women turned their backs on the norms of the day, they seldom came back. She for one never looked back.

She had rebelled against every norm that was imposed on her.

In the most understated manner she had turned the world on its head.

On the eve of the wedding I was still thinking about Madame Sun's funeral. I had no way of relieving the pent-up, bitter feelings inside me.

The most nauseating thing was the picture of Madame Sun in the memorial pamphlet—it showed her all made up, lying in a glass coffin. In front of the coffin stood a group of sad-looking, teary-eyed children in salute position. The caption read, "Children Say Goodbye to Beloved Granny Song." I remembered thinking that she had now been relegated to the position of a grandmother character from a soap opera. What nightmares would the children who had been ordered to stand vigil have that night?

Who really knew her? I was certain no one knew what she thought in her heart of hearts.

She never liked fanfare and had never lived in a traditional family. How could she want a bunch of kids who called her "Granny Song" to shed tears for her?

The concept of family perplexed me as well. Later, when I moved to New York, I dreaded the arrival of December. The streets were crammed with people carrying parcels of all sizes, and fairy lights twinkled everywhere. I lived in a bare old house in Brooklyn that only had a few pieces of old broken furniture. No matter how I moved the furniture around, the room with the backdrop of festive lights seemed like a funeral parlor.

My longing for a home or family started only after I met Simpson. I felt nervous and anxious; in a few hours I would be taking the traditional path.

55

They tried to feed Dr. Sun with a spoon, but the soup dribbled down his chin as soon as his lips closed.

The bloating grew worse; the doctor decided to stop the saline injections he had been prescribing.

56

Before she lost consciousness, her mind calmly contemplated the intricacies of death. Death was like an incredible threshold, not frightening in the least. At the brink of death she felt strangely relaxed, as if her time had finally come. She had severed her ties with the past long before, and through death she could begin her way back again.

She wanted to return to a point in time when anything was possible. The first time she had met Dr. Sun, she was wearing a white A-line shift with a scalloped neckline. Now that death was in sight, she seemed to smell again the sweet scent of that dress all those years ago.

She smiled as the scent surrounded her. Unlike her husband all those years ago, she had no unfinished business. Oh, what about Yuyu and Zenzen, the two sisters who were keeping her company by her bedside? . . . She thought about saying something but thought better of it. She recalled her own parents, who did their utmost to plan the children's future, but where did that get them? They would have never wanted to see the three of them so far apart.

The younger generation will always have their future. She felt bone tired. She was ready to let everything go.

Was she really at peace?

In the last one to two years of her life, Madame Sun had begun contacting her old friends from abroad again. In every letter she spoke of her concern for my sister and me. She was letting them know that we were the only human beings she still cared for.

Perhaps she had already foreseen that we would be evicted on the day of her funeral.

Right from the start people cautioned me to keep my mouth shut when I was abroad. Actually, there was no need to warn me; I wanted to make a clean break from the past.

But try as I might, I could not cut myself completely off from the past, not even through marriage to Simpson. Simpson said one of the reasons he liked me was that my past was written all over my face.

In my dreams I returned to the mansion.

My sister had sent me a videotape of Madame's former residence. I watched the documentary that contained no image of its former host. The lens slowly panned the furniture in the rooms; tourists stepped on the rug and peeked at the fireplace before taking pictures under the shade of a big tree.

The two residences of Song Qingling in Shanghai and Beijing have already been listed as important national heritage sites. The video ends with a drowsy score and an affected narration—a voice suddenly shrieks, "Fly—spread your wings and fly into the blue yonder!"

Madame Sun's heavy body held too many untold stories and secrets. Could she really fly?

Where would she fly to?

Dr. Sun felt the curdle of thick phlegm in his chest, but he lacked the strength to cough it up. The contents of his life seemed to be slowly dissipating from his memory. A few scattered images were his sole hold on the material world. He remembered his close comrades from the revolution days. He saw Lu Haudong, Song Jiaoren, Zhu Zhixing emerge before him; he realized these were the faces of deceased comrades. There was still Charlie Song. . . . Song had been his most ardent supporter for many years, but he never forgave Sun at the end of his life. Even on his deathbed Charlie had lamented that he had never experienced such betrayal, first by his own daughter and then by his best friend. When Dr. Sun opened his eyes, Huang Xing's broad open face appeared before his eyes. Sometimes he was envious that Huang Xing had died at an early age so he did not have to witness the murders, revolts, and assassinations that came later. He had lost his temper when he first heard the saying, "Sun Yat-sen is the person with the ideals, while Huang Xing is the person who makes the ideals concrete." This kind of rhetoric implied that he was only a dreamer and that dreaming was a form of pastime for him. Now, however, as he was about to cross that great divide, he felt no trace of resentment. Perhaps the absence of Huang Xing really made his ideals seem like empty talk. Did Huang Xing still blame him? In the early years Sun had always been too impatient. He believed that if they had initiated their campaign against Yuan a few months earlier, the end result would have been different. His defiance had caused him to set up his own China Revolution Party in Tokyo, and he had cut himself off from Huang.

Looking back, he realized that Huang Xing had indeed been right. They really did not have the military strength to face up to Yuan. Even at this point in time he had no idea what support was still available to him. At the same time these thoughts of failure infuriated him. He remembered that Huang Xing and some other comrades had written a letter to him, warning him to "beware of chasing away the tiger and bringing in the wolf." They really believed that he had signed some secret pact with the Japanese. Their preconceived notion of him was hard to bear. The two of them had not seen eye to eye since their United League days. Discord had started when Dr. Sun had insisted that they use the emblem designed by Lu Haudong for the Nationalist flag. Lu had been his closest ally and had died during the very first uprising. He was only twenty-eight. Could Huang Xing not understand the reasons behind Dr. Sun's sentiment? Most comrades sympathized with Huang Xing on this matter and blamed Dr. Sun for being too stubborn and autocratic. They felt he was too full of himself and had spoken out of line. In the end, who had been right and who had been wrong? Who had been the patriot with the proven instincts? Whose name would be remembered by future generations? At that instant Dr. Sun knew that their marathon would continue after his death, but he would not be able to contribute any more. There would be no way for him to amend past mistakes. What should he do? He was suddenly anxious that he would no longer be able to clean up his record. He remembered his habit of having pieces of paper handy so he could spontaneously jot down his thoughts. Very often the piece of paper would be misplaced after he rolled it around in his hands for some time. Occasionally, when one of the pieces of paper materialized out of nowhere, he would be perplexed at the message he had written. He was not used to keeping a diary or, rather, he had never kept a diary for the sake of future generations. In that case would they understand what he had tried to do? How would people get to know the real him? How could he defend himself? People would see evidence of his revolutionary and nation-building efforts, but they would also see how the lack of real power left China in a messy predicament.

At that second Dr. Sun felt completely disillusioned. He was reminded of his days of drinking and singing at a small pub in Tokyo. He would chant the lyrics "everything in the world is but a dream" out loud. Indeed, the world didn't make much sense. When the curtain came down, it came down for good. Who had written the words to those lyrics? At that moment Dr. Sun saw Miyazaki Toten singing on stage with a fan in one hand. Sun remembered the lines he would often recite: "I abandon the sword to hold a fan, while the *sakura* dies with the last toll of the bell." Thinking of his bearded friend, Sun's brows relaxed and happiness suffused him. He had first laid eyes on him in Yokohama . . . how long ago had that been? Ever since they met, Toten had never turned his back on him and he defended Dr. Sun at every turn. The police authorities in Japan, the Ministry of Foreign Affairs, even Yuan Shikai had tried to bribe Toten, but he had stayed true to Sun despite his impoverishment. He was a man of principle. Toten had always been searching for a hero. That morning . . . suddenly, Dr. Sun felt his pain subside, and he was transported back to the unforgettable memories of friendship and male bonding . . . that morning when he had opened his window and seen for the first time this strong, imposing man standing in the courtyard waiting for him. Dr. Sun had rushed gaily downstairs to meet him.

Later Toten had admitted to Dr. Sun that he had been slightly disappointed upon meeting him in person. Dr. Sun had been wearing his bathrobe, and he had not bothered to brush his teeth or wash his face. In Toten's eyes that was a mark of poor manners. Dr. Sun knew he tended to be coarse at times. A few years before that meeting, the older comrades had criticized him for being slack and careless. Nonetheless, Toten had accepted him and given him his heart. However, Toten had passed away too. Did he find the absolute freedom he longed for in the afterworld?

Sun seemed to be able to hear the sound of funeral bells tolling in the distance. He remembered that he still had some unfinished business to tend to before dying. He tried to collect his thoughts, but his mind wandered to Zijingshan in Nanjing, where he had taken his children hunting before. He remembered the strong gray stallions he had found there. Sun had looked magnificent then. He was the interim president, and even though the position was temporary, it had still been the best period of his life.

The room began to darken; he knew his time was running out. He opened his mouth to speak. It seemed as if he were asking to be buried in Nanjing, at Zijingshan, where he had gone hunting before. He struggled to open his eyes wide; he wanted to see the outcome of so many things. His gamble was not yet over. His position was irreplaceable and his ideology had not been realized yet. He was sure his instincts had been correct and that people supported him after all. He was unwilling to give it all up. . . . An ink pen was placed in his hand and his wife gently supported his wrist. With much effort he signed three different letters, including one that had just been read to him: "I am suffering a terminal illness yet my mind constantly thinks of you . . . as I bid you all farewell, brothers, I wish you peace." The last letter that was handed to him was "A Farewell Message to the Soviet," drafted in English by Chen Yoren and Borodin. Ironically, after it was translated into Chinese, it turned out to be the most emotional letter of the lot.

Everything happened haphazardly during these final moments. No one knew for sure what Dr. Sun's future place in history would be, just as no one knew that it would take death to turn him into a true hero. Even Wang Jingwei, who wrote the first two wills for Dr. Sun, had no way of foreseeing that several months later he would need to recall Dr. Sun's final moments in detail. He would be asked to write a seemingly historical account of what Dr. Sun said. "Dr. Sun half-groaned and half-shouted, 'Peace, struggle, save China!' over and over again, at least forty times." In later generations people questioned how the dying Sun had the energy to say all that. Undeniably, "Peace, struggle, save China!" was a mouthful.

Similarly, as the last tear fell, Sun Yat-sen was unable to stop his comrades from requesting that his corpse be embalmed the way Lenin's had been. Later a needle was injected into his right leg and all his internal organs were removed. The chairman of Xiehe Hospital, Liu Reihuan, personally presided over the operation. A yellow puslike fluid flowed from Sun's body during the process. After it was cleaned up, the workers stuffed the corpse just as a taxidermist stuffs an animal. The prime minister is immortal, just as his spirit will always be immortal! The comrades soaked the body of the foremost hero of the Republic in formaldehyde so people could pay tribute to the man at a later date.

She died smiling. At the last second her sagging neck dropped to one side, and the years rolled by like the soft hue of an old movie. She saw the pretty, youthful face of her youth rising from the dimming lights, then disintegrating into the past. In one scene her youngest brother was still the little boy who kicked his short little legs back and forth as he sat on the heavy redwood chair, waiting for his picture to be taken. In the next scene she was meeting Sun Wen for the first time. She seemed as pure and radiant as a sprig of jasmine, so untainted.

The loves of her life emerged behind her closed eyes. Therein lay her faith. To them she remained loyal to the last; just one look again and she could fall in love with them all over again. She remembered that she had taken the rickshaw to see Dr. Sun. Her skirt had ballooned from the wind; she wanted to get there as quickly as possible.

Her mind began to falter; around her neck an anchor weighed her down. The gold heart-shaped pendant her father gave her shone in the darkness. She reached out, hoping to hold on to Papa's hand. She had let it go only for a brief second all those years before.

Was life and death simply one long road? If she could join the pieces together, would the love she had been searching for be waiting at the other end of the road, in another space and time?

When I moved abroad, I began to have a clearer picture of the entire story. Madame Sun hardly ever told her side of the story, so it was bound to become a legend that later generations could only piece together. The jigsaw lacked a few key parts; the truth about her was buried in an enigmatic sea.

One example: I remember reading an account in a book published by the Song Qingling Foundation about the days preceding her death. It read more like a novel than real life; "One night, a black car sped to her residence behind the lake. The man who got out of the car was Liao Zhongkai's son Liao Chengji. He hurried up the stairs to Song's bedside. In great excitement, he told her the good news—the Central Committee of the Communist Party had agreed to formally accept her as a full member of the Chinese Communist Party."

According to the book, Madame "joyously opened her eyes. Her lifelong wish had been granted. She couldn't stop nodding her head and smiling. She tried to move her lips but she couldn't speak as she was still feverish and in a critical condition.

"The next day, at the 18th meeting of the 5th National Peoples' Congress, Song Qingling was appointed the Honorary President of the People's Republic of China."

Did I miss something? Is this also a piece of the jigsaw puzzle?

Some people professed that they saw a copy of her will that had been leaked overseas through unofficial channels. On the so-called will Madame Sun had written, "The Republic has been established for thirty-one years, but why have the developments been so wayward? There is very little left for me to say and even less for me to do."

Which version reflects what she truly felt?

She had played a joke on us all. She did not leave a will, nor did she say anything definitive, even to the two of us. In the end no one really knew what was on her mind.

Just as a book written in English commented, "Everyone who was there—and not there—claimed they played a very important role at Sun's death."

Madame Song's sister Ailing told many around her that she had stressed on numerous occasions that "my husband, Kong Xiangxi, must assume the permanent responsibility of caring for Song Qingling."

As for Liao Zhongkai's wife, He Xiangning, she later recollected that she had told Dr. Sun that she would do her utmost to protect Madame Sun. Apparently, He Xiangning had sworn that she would never go back on her promise.

Dr. Sun's aide Ma Xiang wrote in an essay commemorating Sun Yat-sen that right at the end, Sun had told his wife, "Ma Xiang has served me all his life. You have to take care of him till his death and support his children until they graduate from university." Late at night on March 11, when Dr. Sun was already unconscious and around the time when Wang Jingwei supposedly heard him call out "Peace, struggle, save China!" Ma Xiang remembered hearing Dr. Sun murmur the words, "Comrades, carry out my beliefs and learn from Russia."

The reason for the divergent versions of Dr. Sun's death could be that almost no first-hand record exists of what took place. History was happening spontaneously. In a column called Correspondence from Beijing and written for the Shanghai newspaper *Shen Bao,* a witness to Dr. Sun's death lamented that his photographic equipment had been destroyed during the war, so he could not take photographs at that moment. He wrote, "I regret that no photographer was present at such an important time. Those present were too grief-stricken to think about keeping records. If my photographic equipment had not been stolen by the Qi faction, at least there would be some pictures for our readers."

Aside from printing Dr. Sun's obituary, which was issued by the Nationalist Party, the newspapers in the North didn't give a great deal of coverage to his passing. In the North, Dr. Sun was not seen as a heavyweight. Many thought he was just an old man, past his prime, who refused to step down. At most they felt a tinge of disconsolation that he had failed as a hero. Most eyes were focused on the imminent Zhongyuan War and the battle between Hu Jingyi and Han Yukun. The headlines on the day that Sun Yat-sen died included news of a lost child, a rebellious young woman, brothel specials, and the ridiculous incident of a dog giving birth to a pig. That day's paper also contained a detailed menu of what the Banchan Lama ate on his first day in Beijing. For breakfast he had cereal, ham, eggs, fried fish, and sautéed beef. The Banchan Lama was preparing to negotiate with Chief Executive Duan to take back Outer Mongolia at the time. There was also some mention of Zhang Xueliang's paying a personal visit to Zhang Zuolin at his hotel to offer up congratulations for Zhang Zuolin's birthday celebrations.

Only on the third day after Sun died did news appear about Chief Executive Duan's agreeing to award $60,000 to Sun Yat-sen for funeral preparations because of his contributions to the Republic. From Russia, Stalin issued a standard message of condolence to China. Stalin himself was jubilant. He had just received news that the leader of the Bolsheviks, General Semenoff, had surrendered. As for other news concerning Dr. Sun in the same newspaper, the main eulogy came from the owner of Ren Dan pharmaceutical company. He spoke of how his friendship with Dr. Sun had begun during the second year of the Republic, when Dr. Sun had visited the company's headquarters in Osaka. He had invited Dr. Sun to his residence, and they had an enjoyable time together, drinking and chatting. The businessman lamented that with Dr. Sun's death, those days were gone. The surprising thing was that the small silver-colored pills that Ren Dan sold could supposedly cure all ills, including sexually transmitted diseases. The trademark on the box, Bo Ai (love), was written in Dr. Sun's handwriting. The small writing on the side of the box specified that Ren Dan could cure syphilis and other venereal diseases. The remote regions of China were still in the dark about Sun's death. In the papers various doctors attempted to find the right medication for Dr. Sun's ailments, boldly prescribing herbs that would speed up circulation and cool down the body, citing these remedies as foolproof.

As for newspapers abroad, the *Times* of London printed the benevolent headline "A Light Extinguished." The article lamented the passing of a man who had suffered countless failures and ultimately sacrificed his own life for the sake of the revolution. The evening papers in Paris criticized Dr. Sun for outdated thinking that never amounted to much. The editorial sections of newspapers in Japan all praised Dr. Sun for his revolutionary spirit. Several prominent newspapers in Tokyo that were adept at predicting future developments wrote that in future the Nationalist Party was destined to split up.

Taiwan, still under Japanese rule, had a memorial service organized by the comrades of the Yozhi Association. Records state that "officers of the Association were summoned to the Police Bureau on the day prior to the service. They were prohibited from singing the memorial song they had composed and banned from reading the already pre-edited eulogy out loud." A complaint lodged in the *Taiwan Min Bao* newspaper published on April 11, 1925, said, "Why can we not sing our song? Why does our eulogy need to be inspected? Can Taiwan not weep on the eve of a great man's death? Why do we have to swallow our tears of sorrow?"

Not long thereafter the newspapers in the North began covering another wave of celebrations. The powerful and the elite had congregated in Yue Zhou, this time to celebrate the birthday of Wu Peifu, which took place at the end of March.

Death is inevitably the end of a journey. Death also allows the journey to go back to the beginning.

I yawned and looked out the window. A new day had broken and a dull gray light glimmered on the horizon.

My eyes followed the blue-and-white striped tent on the lawn. In preparation for this big day, cypress vines braided in a heart shape were entwined around the arch that would be at the end of the runner.

When I step on the rose petals and walk toward Simpson, who will be waiting at the other end for me, I will take on a new name and embark on a new chapter of my life.

I pulled the curtains down as I readied myself for my little nap. I started to shut Madame Sun's book, but I knew her story was far from over. Many people, including me, will continue to look for clues . . . to her life and her times.

Her story will not end with one book.

ABOUT THE AUTHOR

Ping Lu has established herself as a prominent novelist, columnist, and commentator in Taiwan since the mid-1980s. After graduating from the Department of Psychology at National Taiwan University, she pursued advanced studies at the University of Iowa and received her master's degree in mathematical statistics.

Before assuming her current post as director of Kwang Hwa Information and Culture Center in January 2002, she had lectured for many years on such subjects as feminism, cultural criticism, and news commentary at National Taiwan University and Taipei National University of the Arts.

As a professional writer, Lu Ping is very concerned about social issues, cultural development, gender inequality, human rights, and the like. She is also noted for her unflinching support of Taiwan's feminist movement. Although Lu Ping is best known as a novelist in Taiwan, she also writes essays, commentary, and plays. Her novels include *Brother Chuan* and *The Story of Teresa*; among her collections of short stories are *Death in a Cornfield, Letters of Madame Song Meiling, Five Paths through the Dusty World,* and *Apocalypse from the Banned Books*; her critical works include *Not about Chauvinism, Women Power,* and *Women and Love*; and her collections of essays include *Deep in My Mind* and *The Seven Flavored Soups of a Witch.*

Modern Chinese Literature from Taiwan

Wang Chen-ho, *Rose, Rose I Love You*

Cheng Ch'ing-wen, *Three-Legged Horse*

Chu T'ien-wen, *Notes of a Desolate Man*

Hsiao Li-hung, *A Thousand Moons on a Thousand Rivers*

Chang Ta-chun, *Wild Kids: Two Novels About Growing Up*

Michelle Yeh and N.G.D. Malmqvist, editors,
Frontier Taiwan: An Anthology of Modern Chinese Poetry

Li Qiao, *Wintry Night*

Huang Chun-ming, *The Taste of Apples*

Chang Hsi-kuo, *The City Trilogy: Five Jade Disks,
Defenders of the Dragon City, Tale of a Feather*

Li Yung-p'ing, *Retribution: The Jiling Chronicles*

Shih Shu-ching, *City of the Queen: A Novel of Colonial Hong Kong*

Wu Zhuoliu, *Orphan of Asia*